LADY GUNSMITH

9

Roxy Doyle and the Lady Executioner

Books by J.R. Roberts
(Robert J. Randisi)

Lady Gunsmith series
The Legend of Roxy Doyle
The Three Graves of Roxy Doyle
Roxy Doyle and The Shanghai Saloon
Roxy Doyle and The Traveling Circus Show
The Portrait of Gavin Doyle
Roxy Doyle and the Desperate Housewife
Roxy Doyle and the James Boys
Roxy Doyle and the Silver Queen
Roxy Doyle and the Lady Executioner

The Gunsmith series

Angel Eyes series

Tracker series

Mountain Jack Pike series

Coming Soon!
Lady Gunsmith 10
Roxy Doyle and the Queen of the Pasteboards

For more information visit:
www.SpeakingVolumes.us

LADY GUNSMITH

9

Roxy Doyle and the Lady Executioner

J.R. Roberts

SPEAKING VOLUMES, LLC
NAPLES, FLORIDA
2020

Roxy Doyle and the Lady Executioner

ISBN 978-1-64540-172-8

Chapter One

Roxy Doyle heard the shots.

The mare she was riding heard them, too, and got skittish.

"Whoa, easy there," she said, stroking the brown neck. "Let's go and see what that's about."

She rode in the direction of the shots, heard more as she was approaching. Off to her right, she saw a riderless horse cantering away from her. She assumed it belonged to somebody involved with the shooting.

Finally, she came over a rise and saw four or five men—five for sure, she counted—firing at a lone figure who was pinned down behind some rocks.

As she watched, the firing increased. They could have been a posse, but five shooting at one was never a good thing. She doubted that a sheriff was overseeing the action, unless there was nobody in charge. She had often seen a posse go rogue without someone to guide them.

She dismounted, considered she had three choices: One, fire on them, giving the solitary figure time to get away. Two, circle around and come up behind them, try to identify what was actually going on. The third choice was to turn and ride away, and whatever was going to happen, happen.

She didn't like the third option.

Then she thought of a fourth.

She mounted up again, rode down off the rise and circled around to come up behind the lone figure, who appeared to have no horse. She got as close as she dared, then dismounted and, in a crouch, continued on, rifle in hand. The firing continued, and she actually heard bullets fly past her and over her head. It certainly would have been easier to just ride away, but it was too late to change her mind.

When she came within sight of the person, she called out, "Hey, hello!"

The figure turned and Roxy held her hands out to show that they were empty. She was shocked to see a woman who appeared to be in her early thirties, wearing a worn Stetson pulled down tight over dirty blonde hair, a jacket, jeans and boots. She was holding a rifle and pointing it at Roxy.

"I'm here to help," Roxy said.

"You're not with them?" the woman asked.

"I don't even know who they are," Roxy said. "I just saw what was going on and picked a side."

Shooting started again, and Roxy yelled, "You better get down!"

The woman snapped, "Get over here!" then turned and resumed her position behind the rocks. Roxy ran over to join her.

"Who are they?" she asked.

"I don't even know," the woman said. "They rode up on me and started firing."

"Where's your horse?"

"I let him go," she said. "I didn't want him getting hit by flying lead." She waved behind them. "He's back there, somewhere."

"I think I saw him," Roxy said. "A grey roan with a light mane?"

"That's him."

"He didn't look like he was in a hurry."

"Bucky never wanders too far. He's a good boy."

The woman fired her rifle a couple of times, just to return fire.

"Stop shooting," Roxy said.

"What?" the woman asked. "Just let them keep shootin' at me?"

"Yes," Roxy said. "If you don't fire back, they're going to start to wonder if you've been hit."

"So?"

"They'll try to move closer, for a look," Roxy said. "That's when we can pick 'em off."

"I'm not a very good shot," the woman said.

3

"Then you're in luck," Roxy said, "because I am."

***

Across the way several of the five men kept firing, until one of them said, "That's enough!"

They stopped and four of the men turned to face the one who had spoken.

"Why?" one of them asked.

"I wanna see what's goin' on," the spokesman said. "Maybe she got hit."

"Want me to go and have a look, Vance?" another man asked.

"Just wait," Vance Hackett said. "Be patient." He glared at a man named Darius. "If this idiot hadn't started firin' too soon, we mighta had her, but she was able to take cover."

"Sorry, Vance," the young Darius said, "but I thought I hadda clear shot."

"The only clear shot you ever had was at bein' an idiot for the rest of your life," Vance said. "You don't do nothin' unless I tell ya, got it?"

"I got it, Vance," Darius said, with hurt in his eyes.

"And that goes for the rest of you," Vance said. "Nobody fires again unless I say so."

The other men all nodded.

"Now just stay hunkered down," Vance told them, "and watch."

Chapter Two

"What's your name?" Roxy asked.

"Angela Blackthorne," the woman said, peering out toward the five men who had now stopped firing. "And who're you?"

"Roxy Doyle."

Angela looked at Roxy with interest

"I heard of you," she said. "Yeah, all that red hair. What made you stop to help me?"

"I didn't like the odds," Roxy said. "Five-to-one never looks fair to me."

"Five-to-two ain't much better," Angela said, "unless one of the two is Lady Gunsmith." She looked out toward the shooters again. "Do you think you can really pick them off from here?"

"If I have to," Roxy said.

"What do you mean?" Angela asked. "How will we get out of here if you don't?"

"Well," Roxy said, "*I* got here, didn't I. My horse is tied back there a ways. If we get to it, we can get away."

"Ridin' double?" Angela asked. "They'd run us down in no time flat."

"We'd only be riding double until we reached your horse," Roxy said. "And maybe I can give them something to think about, first."

"Without killin' them?" Angela asked.

"I really don't like to kill anyone unless I know they deserve it," Roxy said.

"They *are* tryin' to kill me," Angela pointed out.

"That's true," Roxy said, "and if you want to kill any of them, don't let me stop you."

"Like I said," Angela answered, "I'm a terrible shot. They'd have to get a lot closer."

"Well," Roxy said, "let's give them a little time to make up their minds."

***

"Now what?" one of the men asked. His name was Bask. "We been here a while."

"Let's find out if she was hit," Vance said.

"How do we do that, Vance?" Darius asked.

"*We* don't," Vance said "you and Corbin do. Just creep on up there and see what you can see."

"Huh?" Darius said.

"Come on, kid," Corbin said, glumly. He knew it was useless to argue with Vance once he made up his mind. "I'll show ya how it's done."

7

Corbin broke from their cover, with Darius behind him, and started for the cluster of rocks the woman had been using for cover.

***

"Here comes somebody," Angela said.

"Relax," Roxy said. "I've got this."

"Are you sure?" Angela asked.

Roxy had been ready to fire a few shots their way, but now paused

"Are they a posse?" Roxy asked.

"No."

"Are you wanted for something?" Roxy said. "Are they bounty hunters?"

"No!" Angela said, more forcefully, this time. "I've got no bounty on me. I told you, I don't know why they're after me . . . unless . . ."

"Unless what?"

"They might be tryin' to stop me from gettin' to the next town."

"Which is?"

"Copper City."

Roxy had been through the territory of Arizona before, but had never been to Copper City.

"Is that a mining town?"

"Not that I know of," Angela said. "I think it was named after somebody name Copper."

"Why are you going there?"

Angela hesitated.

"To do a job," she finally said.

"And you think they might be trying to stop you?" Roxy asked.

"It's possible," Angela said.

"Why?"

"Well . . . my job is not a very popular one."

"Do you want to tell me what it is?" Roxy asked. "I can make up my own mind."

"I don't know," Angela said. "It may *change* your mind about wantin' to help me. Can't that wait until we get out of this?"

"I don't think so. I'd like to know, now. It can't be that bad."

"I don't know," Angela said, "you tell me."

Okay, I will," Roxy said, and listened for the answer.

"I'm a hangman."

Chapter Three

"I don't see anything wrong with that," Roxy said, after thinking a moment. "But let's talk about it later."

She settled her elbows on the rock in front of her and watched as two men started to make their way forward. She decided to take the first man's hat off and see what effect that had on their resolve.

She fired, and the man's hat flew from his head. He immediately dropped to the ground, leaving the man behind him confused. Roxy convinced the second man to lie prone by taking his hat off as well. Two shots, two hats.

"That's good shootin'," Angela said.

"Let's see if they want to keep moving forward," Roxy said.

But it became obvious they did not. Both of them remained on their bellies and began to crawl back to the others . . .

***

"She's still there, and she's alive," Corbin said to Vance, as he and Darius got back to cover.

"And she can shoot!" Darius added.

"Lucky shot," Vance muttered.

"Lucky shots," Corbin said. "She did it twice."

"Whatta we do now?" one of the other men said.

"Lemme think," Vance said, but as dumb as the other four men were, they knew that thinking wasn't Vance's strong suit.

***

"Let's move," Roxy said. "Looks like I gave them something to think about. Stay low and back away."

The two women began to inch back, and when Roxy thought they were far enough away, she straightened a bit and began to move faster. Angela followed, and before long they had reached Roxy's mare.

"She's not gonna carry both of us very far," Angela commented.

"She won't have to," Roxy said. "Your horse isn't far." She mounted, slid her rifle into its scabbard, and then reached down. "Come on, let's go!"

Angela let Roxy pull her up behind her, and then they were off.

***

"We're gonna circle around," Vance finally said.

"Who's gonna circle?" Corbin said.

"Me and you, Corbin," Vance said. "Is that all right with everybody?"

It was all right with all of them except Corbin, but he remained silent.

"The rest of you lay down some cover fire to distract her," Vance said. "Ready? Go!"

***

Roxy and Angela heard the shooting, but it faded behind them as they rode. When they spotted Angela's horse, she slid down from behind Roxy and waited while Roxy rode her roan down and brought it back.

"Nice horse," Roxy said, as Angela mounted up.

Roxy remembered spotting the hangman's noose dangling from the saddle when she first saw the horse, and now she knew why it was there.

"I'm ridin' right to Copper City," Angela said. "You want to come along?"

"Why not?" Roxy said. "You might need some more help getting there."

"And I'll buy you supper as a thank you for what you did," Angela offered.

"I'll take you up on that," Roxy said, and the two women rode off, leaving the shots behind them.

***

Vance and Corbin circled around and when they reached the rocks where the hangman had been hiding, saw that she was gone.

"Sonofabitch!" Vance said.

Corbin may have been dumb, but he could read sign.

"Look here," he said, pointing to the ground. "Two different boot tracks. There was two of 'em."

"So she had help," Vance said. "Probably the one who shot your hat off. I figured she wasn't the marksman."

"Whatta we do now?"

"I don't like it," Vance said, "but we gotta go back to Copper City and tell the boss we didn't get 'er."

"Jesus," Corbin said, "he's gonna be mad."

"He sure as hell is," Vance said, and he was already formulating a story that would blame the other four men for the failure.

Chapter Four

Copper City, Arizona was a bustling town, not very large, but apparently very busy. But even with the street filled with horses and wagons, the two women—one with flaming red hair, the other with a hangman's noose hanging from her saddle—attracted attention.

"I have to check in with the sheriff," Angela said.

"We haven't even talked about how you became a hangman," Roxy complained. "Or is it hangwoman?"

"I'm not even sure," Angela said. "I haven't been at it very long. Why don't we discuss it when we have supper? I was told there'd be a room waiting for me at the Sutter House Hotel. Why don't you check-in there, and we can meet in the lobby. Around six?"

"Sounds good," Roxy said. "I'll see you then."

They split up, Angela riding to the sheriff's office, Roxy to the hotel to check-in, and then see to her horse . . .

***

Vance Hackett and his men rode into Copper City soon after. While Vance went to report to his boss, the other four stopped at the Hellion Saloon for beer, whiskey and complaints.

The town of Copper City did, indeed, get its name from the family who founded it forty years earlier. But the current head of the family was not named Copper, but Sughrue. He had become a member of the family by marriage and had risen to the top of the chain of command.

Vance Hackett entered Edward Sughrue's office, his hat in his hand. The man behind the desk was in his sixties, but still vital, with only a slight stoop to his shoulders and sharp, intelligent eyes.

"Tell me you stopped her," Sughrue said.

"Um, we didn't, sir," Vance said.

"What happened?"

"One of the men fired too soon, and then she had help," Vance said.

"From who?"

"That we don't know."

"You know that everyone in this town wants to see my son dance at the end of a rope, right?" Sughrue asked.

"Yessir."

"And you also know that I'm not about to let that happen, right?"

"Yessir."

"So if you didn't stop her, she's here," Sughrue said. "Check the hotel and see who she rode in with. If she has help, I want to know who."

"Yessir."

"Now get out."

"Yessir."

Vance backed out and shut the door.

Sughrue knew he had sent five idiots to stop Angela Blackthorne. He thought that killing her father would give him time to come up with a plan to free his son. After all, hangmen don't grow on trees. He thought it would take the town some time to bring in another. But then, her telegram had arrived saying she'd be taking her father's place and would arrive as planned.

Now it looked like he was going to need somebody smarter, and better to get the job done.

He stood, put on his jacket and hat and left his office . . .

***

Sheriff Larry Homer looked up from his desk as his office door opened. He saw a strong handsome looking woman enter, her manner extremely no nonsense, as she was carrying a rifle like somebody who knew how to use it.

"Sheriff Homer?" she asked.

"That's right." He stood, realized she was taller than he was. Unconsciously, he puffed out his chest, but to no avail. Her presence dominated the room.

"I'm Angela Blackthorne."

"Oh, the hangman's daughter."

"Actually, the hangman, now," she said. "Apparently, somebody in this town thought that killing my father would give your prisoner more time. I'm here to make sure it doesn't."

"Uh, well, he does have a lot of friends and family hereabouts."

"Looks like he didn't have enough to keep him from being convicted and sentenced to hang."

"That's true," Homer said. "None of them were on the jury."

"Well, I just wanted to let you know I'm here, and ready to proceed two days from now—unless you want to move it up."

"That ain't up to me," Homer said. "I think two days is gonna be fine."

"I didn't see a gallows on the way in," she said.

"It's out back," Homer said. "The family managed to exert enough pressure to keep it from being built on Main Street."

"Exactly how much family is there?" she asked.

"A lot," he said. "They're the founders of Copper City, and there's still a lot of them around. But there's also a lot of citizens who want to see them gone. The town council is even discussing changing the name of the town."

"Well, five men tried to bushwhack me on my way here," she said. "So as far as I'm concerned, Bushwhack would be a fine name." She turned and put her hand on the doorknob. "I'm going to see to my horse, check into my hotel, then get a meal. If anyone in this town tries to kill me, I'm going to defend myself." She opened the door. "Just so you know," she said, and left.

Chapter Five

Roxy took care of her horse and registered at the Sutter House Hotel, requesting a room overlooking the alley, not the front of the hotel.

In the room, she tossed her saddlebags onto the only chair and put her rifle on the bed next to her as she sat.

She knew exactly why she had gotten involved in the shooting predicament of Angela Blackthorne. It was because, at that moment, she had no clue where to look for her father, bounty hunter Gavin Doyle, next. It was at times like that, when she had no direction, that she often found herself getting involved in other people's troubles. It was one of the few bad lessons she learned from the Gunsmith, Clint Adams.

Now that she had committed herself to coming to Copper City with Angela Blackthorne, she was determined to get the whole story at supper. Until then she was going to give her bones and backside a little rest, after days in the saddle. She pulled off her boots and reclined on the bed, setting her gunbelt down within easy reach.

***

Angela Blackthorne got herself settled in her room with much the same thoughts. She was going to have to give Roxy Doyle her whole story if she expected Lady Gunsmith to stick around and keep her alive until she got her job done. She owed it to her father, and maybe Roxy would understand that.

She settled back on the bed but couldn't relax until she jammed the back of the wooden chair in the room under the doorknob.

***

When Roxy got down to the lobby at six, Angela was already waiting there, holding her rifle.

"Any trouble?" she asked.

"Not so far," Angela said, "but I'm expecting it. You ready to eat?"

"I'm starving."

"Let's find a place."

"What about here?" Roxy asked.

"I don't want people thinkin' I'm afraid to walk the streets," Angela replied.

"I just meant because I'm *so* hungry I'd rather not have to walk around and look for a place to eat when we're right here."

"All right," Angela said, "if that's what you want."

As it turned out, the hotel dining room had quite a variety of dishes available, so Angela had chicken and Roxy ordered a pork steak. They both ordered a beer with their meal.

"So," Angela said, "you wanted to know why I'm doing this job."

"I'm curious," Roxy said.

"My father was a hangman for many years," Angela said. "He never wanted me to see him at work, but he did show me his ropes, his variety of knots. And it wasn't really something I wanted to do."

"Until?"

"Until he was killed last week," she said.

"To keep him from coming here?"

"That's what I figured," Angela said, "especially after this morning's attack."

"But what's the point of killing the hangman?" Roxy asked. "There'd just be another one."

"That's what I thought," Angela said. "I figured they were trying to buy some time, and I didn't want to give it to them. So I sent a telegram saying I'd be taking my father's place and the hanging would be on schedule."

"And the schedule is?"

"Two mornings from now."

"Then why come early?" Roxy asked. "Aren't you giving them time to kill you, too?"

"Exactly," Angela said. "I want to find out who killed my father."

"Well, letting them kill you isn't the way to do that," Roxy said.

The waiter came with their meals, which suspended the discussion for a few minutes.

"Look," Angela said, "I didn't have any idea that I was going to meet you, but now that I have, I'm asking you to help me."

"To do what?" Roxy asked.

"Stay alive," Angela said, "and hang this man."

"What do we know about the prisoner?"

"That he was found guilty, and sentenced to hang," she said. "My father always said that was all he needed to know."

"But not for me. I need a little more," Roxy said. "Like why somebody is trying to stop you."

Angela hesitated, then said, "Apparently, the guilty man's a member of the founding family, here."

"Ah," Roxy said. "Now I get it. Have you met the sheriff?"

"I have."

"And?"

"I don't have an opinion yet," Angela said. "It seems as though he's been the law here for some time."

"So it remains to be seen if he's sheriff in name only, or an actual lawman."

"I suppose so." Angela put her fork down and looked at Roxy. "Will you help me, Roxy?"

"I've been looking for my father for a long time," Roxy said. "I don't even know if he's alive."

"I'm sorry," Angela said. "I don't want to keep you—"

"My point is," Roxy said, cutting her off. "that I'll help because of your father. I'll help you see this through, for him, Angela."

"Thank you, Roxy," Angela said. "And since you're going to help me, you might as well start calling me Angie."

Chapter Six

When Edward Sughrue needed a job done with smarts and savvy, he used a man named Kirk.

"Have a seat," Sughrue said to Kirk, as the younger man entered.

Kirk nodded and sat. He was in his forties, dressed in a grey suit, with a holstered gun on his left hip. He removed his Stetson, crossed his legs and put the hat on his knee.

"I got word you wanted to see me," he said, in a deep, gravelly voice. "Is this about Jerry?"

"It is."

"Do you want me to get him out?"

"I'm still trying legal channels," Sughrue said. "I want him out, but I don't want him on the run."

"I understand. What about the hangman?"

"We stopped him," Sughrue said, "but his daughter is here to do his job."

"His daughter?" Kirk raised both eyebrows. "A hang . . . woman?"

"Apparently," Sughrue said.

"What do you want done?"

"I want to talk with her," Sughrue said. "Keep Vance and the others away from her. They're idiots."

"Yes, they are."

"If you can," Sughrue said, "see if you can get her to come and talk to me willingly."

"And if not willingly?"

"Let's try that, first," Sughrue said. "Also, according to Vance, she had help getting away from them. I want to know who. Talk to the sheriff."

"Sure," Kirk said, sarcastically, "he'll be a big help."

"She probably went to him first and is going to want a look at the gallows."

"Undoubtedly," Kirk said, "if she knows her job."

"I need to take her measure," Sughrue said. "And soon."

Kirk nodded and stood, but hesitated before leaving.

"I could just kill her," he said.

"Let's wait and see if that's necessary," Sughrue said. "Get back to me soon."

"Right."

Kirk left. Sughrue sat back in his chair. It was Tuesday afternoon. His son was scheduled to hang Thursday morning. If he couldn't get that decision legally reversed, he would have to let Kirk do what he did best.

He stood and left his office. He had an appointment with Judge Samuel Tyler, the man who had tried and sentenced his son.

***

After supper Angie told Roxy she wanted to have a look at the gallows.

"The sheriff said it's behind the jail," she went on.

"Then let's take a walk," Roxy said. "We might as well be seen together, and let people make of that what they want."

As they approached the sheriff's office Roxy said, "Let's just go in the back and have a look, without the sheriff."

"No problem," Angie said, "since I already saw him once."

They circled the sheriff's office to the back, where they saw the gallows. It was a simple wooden scaffold, with five steps leading up to where the noose would be.

Angie went up the steps, while Roxy remained on the ground. She walked around the platform, feeling it beneath her boots.

"Solid," she said. "Well built."

Roxy walked around the base, touching it every so often.

"Same here," she called back.

Angie walked to the trapdoor in the floor of the platform.

"I'll have to test it," she said. "I can do that tomorrow."

While Angie was walking back down, the sheriff came out of his office.

"I thought I heard voices," he said, as Angie reached the ground.

"I'll have to come back here in the morning and test this structure," Angie told him. "I'll need some sandbags of various weights."

"I'll arrange to have them here," Sheriff Homer said. "And who is this pretty lady?"

"This is Roxy Doyle," Angie said. "She kept me from getting killed this morning."

"Roxy . . . Doyle?"

"Also known as Lady Gunsmith," Angie added.

"Ah," Homer said, "I knew I recognized the name. Yeah, and all that red hair. What brings Lady Gunsmith to Copper City?"

"Keeping Angie alive," Roxy said.

"Is that all?" Homer asked. "Or are you here lookin' for somebody?"

"Like who?"

He shrugged.

"Somebody to kill?" he asked.

"I don't aim to kill anybody," Roxy said, "unless they try to kill me, or Angie."

"I hope that's true, Miss Doyle," Sheriff Homer said. "I hope that's true."

Chapter Seven

Copper City had no Mayor.

Instead they had something called a "City Manager" and at the present time that was Edward Sughrue. But his position wasn't helping him when he had to deal with Judge Tyler.

"Have a seat, Edward," Tyler said. He was white-haired and pink skinned with faded blue eyes. During the trial Sughrue had been praying the man would die of old age before he could sentence his boy.

"If this is about Jerry, I've told you before, you're wasting your time."

"Judge—Samuel—I just need a little more time."

"To do what, Edward?" the Judge asked. "Buy a witness?"

"The hangman rode in today, and it's a woman," Sughrue said.

"I knew she was coming," the Judge said. "Apparently, someone killed her father. You wouldn't know anything about that, would you, Edward?"

"Not a thing," Sughrue said. "But Judge, I can't have my boy hung by a woman!"

"So you're not so worried about him hanging," the Judge said, "you just don't want it at the hands of a woman?"

"I don't want him to hang at all," Sughrue insisted. "He's my only boy, my only family. Once he's gone—"

"There'll be no more Coppers to take up for you," the Judge said. "I know the story, Edward. Your family has meant a lot to this town, but it's time to move on, don't you think?"

"Not if it means losing my boy," Sughrue said.

"Edward, I'm, sorry," the Judge said. "There's nothing I can do. A jury found him guilty. And we *all* know he's guilty. Even you know that."

"He's twenty years old, goddamnit!" Sughrue said.

"Somebody should've been making sure he learned right from wrong, Edward," the Judge commented. "I think, as his father, that should've been you."

Sughrue stood up, angrily.

"Judge, you're going to make me do something I don't want to do?"

"You mean something worse than killing a hangman?" the Judge asked.

"I told you I wasn't behind that!" Sughrue snapped. "But there's no telling what a father will do to save his only son."

"Don't do anything to disgrace your position as City Manager, Edward," the Judge advised.

"Being City Manager is the least of my worries, Judge," Sughrue said, and stormed out.

The Judge thought that last statement was very telling, since he and the town council had already been discussing how to get Sughrue out and vote in a Mayor.

***

It was getting dark, so Angie decided to go back to her hotel.

"I'll come with you," Roxy said.

"Don't you want to check out the saloons in town?" Angie asked.

"Is that what you'd normally do when you come to a town for a hanging?" Roxy asked.

"Don't forget, this is my first," Angie answered.

"Then how about we both go to a saloon and have a beer, just to show the folks here in Copper City that you're a regular person."

"Somebody might also try to put a bullet in me," Angie added.

"Well, that's what I'm here to keep from happening, right?" Roxy asked.

"Right," Angie said. "Let's go."

31

***

They decided not to go to the largest or smallest saloon in town. The one they chose was called The Ace Queen.

"Why not the Ace *and* Queen?" Angie wondered, as they stood in front of the place.

"Who knows?" Roxy said. "As long as they serve beer."

They entered and went straight to the bar. Two women entering together, both armed, attracted attention, which they ignored.

"Two beers," Roxy said to the bartender.

"Are you sure you ladies wanna be in here?" the man behind the bar asked.

"We're sure," Roxy said.

"Aw, go ahead," a man at the bar said, "go ahead and serve the pretty ladies, Lou."

Roxy looked at him. He was in his twenties, with a prominent Adam's apple.

"Thanks," Roxy said, "but we don't need any help."

"Hey, sorry," the young man said. "Just tryin' to help."

The bartender put their beers on the bar.

"Thanks," Roxy said.

"You know," Angie said over her mug, "the men who bushwhacked me this morning might be in here."

"Good," Roxy said, "then they know you're not afraid, and they know we're together." She held up her glass. "Cheers."

***

"Do you see what I see?" Darius asked.

Corbin turned in his chair to have a look.

"Jesus Christ!" he said. "That's her, ain't it?"

"It sure looks like her," Darius said. "Should we take 'er?"

"Who's that with her?" Corbin wondered.

"Who knows?" Darius said. "Just some girl. Come on, we can take 'em."

The two men were sitting together at a table. None of the other men they'd been with that morning when they bushwhacked "the hangman" were with them.

"You know what Vance said," Corbin told the younger man. "Don't do nothin' til we hear from him."

"Yeah, but he don't know she's here," Darius said. "Come on, if I go over there, you'll back my play, right?" He started to get up.

"No, Darius, wait—" Corbin snapped, but it was too late. The young man was striding over to the bar. Against his instincts, Corbin rushed to follow him.

Chapter Eight

Roxy saw the young man purposefully walking toward them and the older one rushing to catch up to him.

"I think you were right," she said to Angie. "I'm thinking those two are bushwhackers."

Angie turned and looked.

"Only two," she said. "What do we do?"

"Relax," Roxy said. "Let them call the play. If something happens, the sheriff'll need to know we didn't start it."

They both turned back to the bar.

"Hey, you!" the young man snapped. "I'm talkin' to you."

Roxy and Angie both turned to look at him. Roxy could tell by the way he wore his gun that he didn't know the first thing about using it. Then she saw the hole in his hat, and also in the hat of the other man as he caught up.

"Ladies," the second man said, "forgive my friend, he's a little drunk."

"How'd you get those holes in your hat?" Angie asked them.

"What?" the older man asked.

"Those holes in your hats," Angie said. "They look fresh. That from this morning, when you bushwhacked me?"

Angie's rifle was on the bar, and she put her hand on it.

The other men at the bar knew something was happening, and they backed away.

"Now wait—" Corbin said.

Roxy stepped between Angie and the two men.

"That's a good idea, friend," she said. "Everybody just take a breath and wait."

It hurt the younger man's ego that both women were taller than he was.

"You got no right comin' here ta hang an innocent man," he snapped.

"Now, whoa there," Roxy said to him. "Innocent men don't get tried and sentenced to hang, do they?"

"Well, this one did," the young man said, "and we ain't gonna let it happen."

"You know," Roxy said, "I put those holes in your hats as a warning. I could've shot lower."

"That was you?" the other man said, suddenly recognizing her. He put his hand on the young man's gun arm. "Darius, I know her. That's Lady Gunsmith."

"I don't care—"

"Listen to your friend," Roxy advised. "I promised the sheriff I wouldn't kill anybody unless they forced me. You look as if you're about to make me fulfill that promise."

"Listen, you bitches—"

Roxy slapped the young man across the face. The saloon was so quiet the sound of flesh-on-flesh reverberated through the room. He looked stunned as he lifted his hand to his cheek.

"You need to learn some manners, Darius!" she snapped at him. She looked at the older man. "What's your name?"

"Um, C-Corbin."

"Mr. Corbin, you better take your young friend out of here before it's too late."

"Yes, Ma'am." Corbin reached out and clamped his hand on Darius' gun arm. "Come on, Darius!" He started pulling him toward the doors.

"And tell your other bushwhacking friends that we're here," Roxy said.

She turned her back but could see both men in the mirror behind the bar. Darius yanked his arm away from Corbin and screamed, "You bitch!"

Roxy turned and drew in the same motion. When she fired, the bullet shattered Darius' forearm, and his gun hand went totally limp before he could draw.

"Ahhh!" he screamed, grabbing his arm with his other hand.

"You're lucky I wanted to keep my promise to the sheriff, Darius," she told him. Then she looked at Corbin and said, "You better get him to a doctor before he loses that arm."

She turned back to the bar.

Chapter Nine

Kirk was standing at the batwings looking in when the sheriff appeared.

"I heard there was a shootin'," he said. "What happened?"

"Is that red haired gal who I think she is?" Kirk said, instead of answering the question.

Sheriff Homer looked in.

"That's Roxy Doyle," he said, "the Lady Gunsmith."

"That's what I thought."

Homer backed away from the batwings.

"What happened?"

"She taught some young pup a lesson."

"Did she kill 'im?"

"No," Kirk said, "she may have shattered his arm, though. His friend took him to the doctor."

"Damn," Homer said, "am I gonna have to run her out of town?"

Kirk turned and looked at Homer, his face betraying his amusement.

"Do you think you could?"

"No," Homer said, honestly, "but I bet you could. How about I deputize you?"

"Sorry," Kirk said, "I already have a job."

"Mr. Sughrue?"

Kirk nodded.

"Are you gonna kill her and the, uh, hang-lady?"

"Don't know yet what I'm going to do, Sheriff," Kirk said, "but why don't you leave this to me and go back to your office?"

"That sounds like a good idea, Kirk," Homer said. "It's all yours."

The sheriff hurried away, and Kirk walked into the bar.

***

"I think we should go before somebody else gets brave," Roxy said. "We made our point."

"Sounds good to me," Angie said.

As they turned, they both saw the tall, handsome man enter, wearing a gun on his left hip like he knew how to use it.

"Oh my," Angie said, under her breath.

He smiled and approached them. Roxy knew how Angie felt. The look of the man was reaching down inside her, probably because it had been a while since she'd been with somebody.

"You ladies aren't leaving, are you?" he asked. "I thought I'd buy you both a drink."

"Well—" Angie said.

"Who are you?" Roxy asked.

"My name is Kirk," he said. "I've been asked to speak to you."

"About?" Roxy asked.

He looked at Angie and said, "About this lady's business. Is your name Blackthorne?"

"It is," Angie said.

Then he looked at Roxy.

"And I know who you are," he said, "especially after what you just did to that kid. Why didn't you kill him?"

"It wasn't necessary to make my point," she answered.

"It might have made it more firmly," he commented.

"I think it did the job."

"So how about it?" Kirk asked. "One drink?"

Before Roxy could answer Angie said, "Why not?"

"And why don't we take them to a table?"

"It's pretty crowded in here," Roxy said.

"Somehow," he said, "I don't think that's going to be a problem."

***

Kirk turned out to be right, but Roxy didn't know if several tables opened up to them because of what she had done, or because of Kirk.

"Hi Kirk," one of the pretty young saloon girls came over and greeted. "What'll you have, handsome?"

"Beers?" he asked Roxy and Angie, and they both nodded. "Three beers, Mandy."

"Comin' up." When the girl turned to walk away, her hip bumped his shoulder.

At that moment, Angie took off her hat and her hair tumbled down to her shoulders. It was the first time Roxy had seen her without the hat jammed down on her head, and she hadn't realized how truly pretty a woman she was. She kept her own hat on.

"What you did was impressive," Kirk said to Roxy.

"You saw?" Angie asked.

"From the doorway."

"I wasn't facing much," Roxy pointed out. "He wasn't even wearing his gunbelt properly."

The saloon girl came with their beers, rubbed her hip against Kirk's shoulder again as she set them down.

"Anythin' else, sweetie?" she asked him.

"We'll let you know if there is," Angie told her.

She gave Angie a dirty look and flounced away.

"Okay, Kirk," Roxy said, "what's on your mind?"

Chapter Ten

"I wanted to warn you," Kirk said.

"About what?" Angie asked.

"Jerry Sughrue has a lot of friends in town."

"Jerry . . . who?" Angie asked.

"I can't believe you're going to hang a man, and you don't know his name."

"Names are really not necessary," she said. "In fact, I prefer not to personalize my . . ."

". . . victims?" he asked.

"Subjects," Angie corrected.

"Is that what they are? The men you hang? Subjects?" Kirk asked.

Roxy noticed Angie wasn't telling Kirk this was her first "subject."

"Would you introduce yourself to someone you're executing?" Roxy asked.

"Actually, I don't know. I've never executed a man."

"Have you killed a man?"

"A time or two," Kirk admitted.

"Ever kill someone you didn't know?" she asked. "A stranger?"

"I get your point," Kirk said, "but when someone's trying to kill you, you defend yourself. You don't introduce yourself. This situation's a little different."

"Nevertheless," Angie said, "I'll be doing my job."

"Will you talk to him first?" Kirk asked.

"I'll have to take my measurements," she told him, "after I test the gallows."

"And you'll be doing that tomorrow?"

"Since he's scheduled to hang the day after," she said, "yes."

"Are you one of them?" Roxy asked.

"One of . . . what?" he asked.

"You said this Jerry has friends," she said. "Are you one of them?"

"Oh, no," he said, "I can't stand the kid."

"Why not?" Angie asked.

"He's a privileged little snot," Kirk said. "Just the kind I can't stand."

"But you work for his father, right?" Roxy asked.

"I do, sometimes," Kirk said. "I also work for other people."

"But right now, you work for his father. What's his name?" Angie asked.

"Edward Sughrue," Kirk said.

"And what's his business?" Roxy asked.

"Among other things, he's the City Manager."

"What's that?" Roxy asked.

"It's what we have instead of a Mayor."

"There's no Mayor, here?" Angie asked.

"No," Kirk said.

"Town Council?" Roxy asked.

"Oh, yeah, we have that," Kirk said. "And we have a Judge, the one who sentenced Jerry Sughrue to hang."

"Was it . . . personal?" Roxy asked. "Did the Judge have something against the Sughrue family."

"It's not really the Sughrue family," Kirk said. "It's the Copper family, but they're all that's left."

"So when Jerry dies, Edward is the only one left?" Roxy asked.

"That's right," Kirk said. "He was hoping Jerry would have kids and continue the family line. But I guess that won't happen now, unless . . ."

"Unless what?" Angie asked.

"Unless the boy doesn't hang."

"And how would that happen?" Roxy asked.

"Edward's trying all the legal channels he can think of," Kirk explained.

"And you killed my father, just to try to make some time?" Angie asked.

"Whoa, Miss," Kirk said, "I didn't kill your father. I don't know who did. I don't even know if it was ordered by Edward."

"Who else would order it?" Angie asked.

"I don't know," Kirk said, "but why would Edward be working legally if he thought just killing the hangman would work?"

"I don't know," Angie said, "but I intend to find out."

"So you plan to do more than just hang Jerry while you're here?" Kirk asked. "You want to find out who killed your father?"

Roxy put her hand on Angie's arm to keep her from saying anymore, even though she thought they might have already said too much.

"All right," Kirk said, "I get it. Whoever did it, or ordered it, you don't want to warn them."

He drained his beer mug and stood up.

"Ladies, it's been a pleasure," he said. "I hope to see you both again before you leave."

He turned and left.

"Now that's a handsome man," Angie said.

"And very well-spoken and mannered for a gunman," Roxy said.

"You really think he's a gunman?"

"Oh yeah," Roxy said, and drank her beer.

Chapter Eleven

Kirk went from the saloon to Edward Sughrue's office, because he knew the man kept late hours.

"Oh, it's you," Sughrue said, after unlocking the door. "You got something for me?"

"You got a drink for me?" Kirk asked.

"Come on in."

Sughrue led the way.

"Whiskey or sherry?" he asked.

"Whiskey," Kirk said, taking a seat.

Sughrue poured Kirk a whiskey, handed it to him, then poured himself a sherry and sat behind his desk.

"What've you got?"

Kirk sipped his whiskey, then said, "Lady Gunsmith."

"What about her?"

"She's in town," Kirk said, "keeping the executioner alive."

"Executioner?"

"Well, she's not a *hangman*, and *hangwoman* just doesn't sound right."

"So we're talkin' about Blackthorne's daughter?"

"That's right."

"She hired a fast gun to keep her alive?"

"Don't know if hired is the right word, but she's here," Kirk said.

"That presents a problem," Sughrue said. "Can you handle her?"

Kirk regarded the whiskey glass in his hand before answering.

"I think it would be . . . interesting," he said.

"Well, you've got about thirty-six hours to figure it out," Sughrue said. "I don't want my boy walking to those gallows."

"No luck with the Judge?"

"That sonofabitch, he wants to hang my boy!" Sughrue snapped. "Once we take care of Blackthorne and Lady Gunsmith, and get my boy free, he's next on my list."

"You're going to want me to kill a judge?" Kirk asked.

"You got a problem with that?" Sughrue asked.

"Not for the right price."

"Then why don't you figure out how you're going to handle those two women," Sughrue said, "and then we'll go from there."

Kirk finished his whiskey and set the glass on Sughrue's desk.

"Wait!" Sughrue said, as Kirk started for the door.

"What?"

"What did you think of those two women?" Sughrue asked.

"Blackthorne was pretty, Lady Gunsmith might be the most beautiful woman I've ever seen."

"That's not what I meant," Sughrue said. "How determined are they?"

"Oh, they're determined," Kirk said. "I didn't sense an ounce of weakness in either of them. Blackthorne is intent on hanging Jerry, and Doyle's just as intent on keeping her alive to do it."

"Damn it!" Sughrue said. "Goddamn women!"

"Yeah," Kirk said, and left.

***

Roxy and Angie went back to their hotel to get some sleep. They considered sleeping in the same room, but then they both decided to simply barricade themselves in their own.

Roxy grabbed the wooden chair in the room and jammed the back of it beneath the doorknob. Angie did the same in her room.

"What if somebody decided to break into our rooms?" Angie asked.

"Sleep with your rifle next to you," Roxy said. "At the first sound of a shot I'll be with you."

"And vice versa," Angie said. "But what if they come for both of us at the same time?"

"I don't think they can get that kind of an attack put together tonight," Roxy said. "They'll need tomorrow to gather that many men."

"So at least we can get one night's sleep," Angie said.

"We'll meet downstairs for breakfast in the morning," Roxy said, "and then go and do your tests."

"Sounds good," Angie said, and that was when they went to their own rooms.

***

Kirk had a room in one of the smaller hotels in town. It had all he needed, which was a chest of drawers and a bed. When he got there, the saloon girl, Mandy, was waiting in his bed, naked.

"Well," she said, "there you are."

"Where'd you think I'd be?" he asked.

"I thought maybe you got a better offer from one of those women," Mandy said. "The one with the red hair was . . . gorgeous."

"Yes, she was," Kirk said, approaching the bed.

"You didn't have to agree with me," she pouted, lying on her back.

He reached down and ran his hands over her bare flesh. She closed her eyes and sighed as his palms found her nipples.

"Don't you worry about those two, Mandy," Kirk said. "Don't you worry, at all."

Chapter Twelve

In the morning, Roxy met Angie in the lobby and they decided to leave the hotel this time for their meal. They walked a couple of blocks, attracting attention as they went, possibly for how they looked, or because of the rope Angie was carrying, with the noose at the end of it.

They walked until they found a small café and went inside. The other diners stared as they walked to a table and sat.

"Do you think the word's gone out about who we are?" Angie asked.

"It might have," Roxy said. "If not, I think it will by the end of the day."

"If Edward Sughrue wants to keep me from hanging his son, he'll have to do something today. Although I still don't see the sense in killing the executioner. There'll just be another one."

"Unless killing both you and your father gives him enough time to get his son released, legally."

"And how would he accomplish that, I wonder?" Angie asked.

"By getting the judge to overrule himself, or some- one else to do it."

"He'd have to get a federal judge to do that, which means sending telegrams or actually going to Topeka, which he doesn't have time to do," Angie reasoned.

Roxy nodded. "And that brings us back to killing you. And to kill you, they'd have to kill me."

"I think without you I would've been dead last night," Angie said. "Those idiots in the saloon, or even Kirk—"

"Kirk is going to try me," Roxy said.

"How do you know?"

"I can tell," Roxy said. "It's the kind of man he is— all the men who think they're fast with a gun, have to test themselves."

"It'd be a shame to kill a hunk of man like that," An- gie said. "I mean, before enjoying him."

Roxy laughed.

"I know what you mean. It's been a while for me."

"Me, too," Angie said, "but unfortunately, I've got other things on my mind."

A waiter came over and they each ordered ham-and- eggs and coffee. The waiter was a young man who couldn't stop staring at Roxy.

"He's in love with you, already," Angie said.

"Then maybe he'll bring us some buttered biscuits."

Moments later, the young waiter came running from the kitchen, carrying a basket of biscuits.

"Here you go ladies," he said, setting the basket down. "I'll be right back with your eggs."

He trotted back to the kitchen, ignoring the waves from diners at other tables.

"You must always get service like this," Angie said, grabbing a biscuit. "I have no idea what it must be like to be as beautiful as you."

"Sometimes," Roxy said, "it causes more problems than it's worth."

The waiter came out with two plates loaded with ham-and-eggs.

"But not today," Angie observed, with a smile.

***

After a hearty breakfast, the two women walked over to the back of the sheriff's office. Sandbags Angie had said she would need were piled near the base of the steps.

"I'm going to need help carrying them up," Angie said to Roxy.

"Ain't that why I'm here?" Roxy asked. "To help?"

They spent the next hour or so hauling sandbags up to the platform, tying them to Angie's rope and then dropping them through the trapdoor.

Sitting on the second step together and catching their breath Roxy said, "So? What's the verdict?"

"It'll do."

"What's next?"

"We have to go into the jail and get the prisoner's measurements and weight."

"Do we have to get a scale?"

"No," Angie said, "my father always did it with the naked eye, taught me to guess a man's weight to within a pound."

"That must be helpful when choosing a lover," Roxy said.

They both laughed.

"I can tell you that Kirk looked like a nice, ripe two hundred pounds of man meat," Angie told her, and they laughed again.

"Sounds like you want to get his measurements before you leave town," Roxy observed.

"Are you kidding?" Angie asked. "The way he was looking at you, I wouldn't stand a chance."

"You know," Roxy said, "some men simply prefer blondes over redheads."

"Maybe," Angie said, laughing, "but not when the redhead is you."

Chapter Thirteen

They entered the sheriff's office together, surprising the man who seemed to have been dozing.

"Can I help you ladies?" he asked, his feet dropping down off his desk.

"I need to see your prisoner, Sheriff," Angie said. "I've got to get some measurements."

"Oh, yeah," he said, "for tomorrow. You, uh, found them sandbags I left back there for you?"

"We did," Angie said. "Thank you."

Homer stood, grabbed the keys from a wall peg, and led them into the cell block.

"You can't go in there with that rifle," he told Angie.

She turned and handed the rifle to Roxy. Homer unlocked the cell door, then backed away.

"What's goin' on?" the young man asked.

He was younger than Roxy had expected, barely twenty from the look of him. He was tall, but slender, and stood respectfully as Angie entered the cell.

"This is your hangman, kid," Homer said.

"What?" Jerry Sughrue seemed shocked. "A woman is gonna hang me?"

"That wouldn't be the case if your father hadn't killed my father," Angie told him.

"Now, you don't know that for a fact," Sheriff Homer said.

"Yes, I do." Angie entered the cell. "Just stand still."

"What're you—oh," he said, when he saw her tape measure.

She measured his height first, then went around his neck. Then she stood back to assess his weight.

"All right," she said, stepping from the cell, "that's it."

"You ain't even gonna talk to me?" the kid complained. "Ain't I even a person?"

"Not to me," Angie said. "You're just a job I'm being paid to perform."

Homer locked the door and left the cellblock with Angie. Roxy watched the boy sit back down on his cot, thought maybe she should say something, but didn't know what. He looked up, saw her watching him.

"You gonna be there tomorrow?" he asked.

"Probably."

"Good," he said, "least I get to look at a pretty woman when they hang me."

Roxy left the cell block. Out in the office she returned Angie's rifle.

"I heard you had some trouble in the saloon last night," Homer said.

"Nothing Roxy couldn't handle," Angie said.

"I expected to see you there after it was all over," Roxy said.

"I heard it was a fair fight."

"Hardly," she said. "That boy shouldn't even be allowed to wear a gun."

"Who was it?" the lawman asked.

"I heard somebody call him Darius," Roxy said. "He and his friend were two of the bushwhackers who tried to kill Angie."

"You know that for a fact?" he asked.

"I can identify the hole I put in each of their hats," she said.

"That won't hold up in court."

"I know it," she said. "But it was them."

"If they try anything again," Angie said, "it'll be more than their hats that gets holes in them."

"Look," Homer said, "you're gonna hang this kid tomorrow, and then be on your way, right? Let's not have any trouble."

"Trouble?" Roxy repeated. "That's up to other people, Sheriff, not us."

"I'll have two deputies with me tomorrow morning, for the hangin'," Homer said. "Is that gonna be enough?"

"You'd know that better than we would, Sheriff," Angie said.

"Two deputies it is, then," Homer said. "And there'll be spectators, of course."

"Of course," she said. "We'll see you tomorrow morning."

Angie and Roxy left the sheriff's office.

Roxy almost said, "That poor boy," but decided not to. She didn't think Angie would appreciate it.

"Lunch?" Angie asked. "All those sandbags, I've worked up an appetite."

"Lunch it is," Roxy said.

***

Kirk entered the sheriff's office after Roxy and Angie had left.

"She get it all done?" he asked.

"Sandbags and measurements," Homer said. "She's all ready. Even has her own rope."

"Very professional."

"Kirk, what're you gonna do?" Homer asked. "You can't interfere with a legal hangin'."

"Oh, I'm aware of that, Sheriff," Kirk said. "You know I'd never do anything . . . illegal."

Homer almost said, "Unless you were paid to," but kept his mouth shut.

Chapter Fourteen

Once again, over lunch, they attracted a lot of attention.

"I think it's you," Roxy said, once they had their steak sandwiches.

"No, the men are looking at you," Angie argued.

"Either way, we're being watched."

"Do you think the bushwhackers will try again?" Angie asked.

"They weren't very good at it, were they?" Roxy asked. "No, I think it's more likely Kirk will try something."

"That's too bad," Angie said. "It'd be a shame to kill a man as handsome as he is."

"That's going to be up to him," Roxy said. "Or whoever he's working for."

"Sughrue, probably," Angie said. "The old man's got to make a try at getting his boy out sometime today, or tonight."

"Unless he leaves it until the last minute."

"Do you think we should just wait and see?" Angie asked. "Or force the issue."

"Force it how?" Roxy asked.

"What if we go and see him?" Angie suggested.

"And do what? Kill him?"

"I'd like to," Angie said, "but I wouldn't ask you to do that. And I wouldn't do it. Not in cold blood, anyway."

"So what, then? Just talk to him?"

"Maybe," Angie said, "I can get him to make another try at me. If we can prove he killed my father, and tried to kill me, maybe we can make tomorrow a two for one hanging."

"That'd be up to the judge, I suppose," Roxy said.

"Then maybe we should talk to him," Angie said.

"You should be doing that, anyway," Roxy said. "I figure he'll be at the hanging tomorrow, to see that it goes off without a hitch. I'm sure he'd like to meet you."

"That's an idea," Angie said. "Let's go straight there from here."

"You could even show him your rope," Roxy said, looking down at the noose at Angie's feet.

"I like the sound of this more and more," Angie said, picking up her sandwich.

***

After lunch, they walked to the building which was the courthouse and City Hall.

"Why do they need a City Hall if they don't have a Mayor?" Angie wondered aloud.

"It's pretty new," Roxy said. "Things may be on the verge of changing."

As Angie opened the door and started to enter, Roxy held back.

"What's wrong?" Angie asked.

"I just realized," Roxy said, "we don't know who Jerry Sughrue killed, how or why."

Angie stepped back and allowed the door to close.

"I don't have to know that to do the job, Roxy," she said. "That's one thing my father told me a long time ago. There would be no way he could do the job unless he maintained his objectivity. He never asked questions. All he had to know was that the prisoner had been sentenced to hang."

"That makes sense," Roxy said. "I guess I just have too much curiosity to ever do your job."

"You could've killed Darius last night without knowing much about him," Angie pointed out.

"But I didn't," Roxy said, "and I was wrong."

"Why?"

"Because when you're facing a man with a gun, you have no idea how fast or accurate he is. That means you have to do your level best all the time and shoot to kill."

"But you didn't," Angie pointed out. "Not last night, and not yesterday."

"Like I said, I was wrong, both times. Moreso yesterday, but I didn't know who they were, or who I would've been killing. At that moment you still could've lied to me, and they could've been a posse."

"And last night?"

"That was different," Roxy said. "I could plainly see that Darius had no idea what he was doing. I would never take a chance like that with Kirk."

"Why not?"

"You just have to look at Kirk, the way he wears his gun, the way he moves, to realize he knows how to use it. If I end up going against him, it's going to be shoot to kill for both of us."

"Well, that may be," Angie said, "but I'm not even gonna ask who this boy killed, or what his motive was supposed to have been. I'm just gonna hang 'im. And when I do it, I hope somebody feels the way I did when my dad died."

That said, she opened the door to the City Hall building and entered.

Roxy hesitated, looked up and down the street. There were people on both sides, going about their business. But no one seemed to be paying any attention to them at that moment.

Finally, she followed.

Chapter Fifteen

Judge Samuel Tyler looked up from his desk as his clerk showed the two women into his chambers.

"What can I do for you ladies?" he asked.

"Just wanted to introduce myself, Judge," Angie said. "I'm Angela Blackthorne, your hangman for tomorrow."

"Ah yes," he said, "I understand your father was killed and you're standing in for him."

"That's right."

"You have my sympathies, but are you sure this is a profession for a lady?"

"I'm not all that sure I can say it's my profession," Angie replied. "But I'm going to make sure this hanging goes off without a hitch, since somebody must've thought they could put it off by killing my father."

"Are you accusing anyone in particular?" he asked.

"I could point to the prisoner's father," Angie said, "but, no, I can't prove he had the deed done. I just feel it in my heart."

"And so you want to hang his son in reprisal," Judge Tyler said.

"No reprisal," Angie said. "The law said the boy has to hang, my father was set to do it. I'm just seeing it through."

"And you?" Tyler said, looking at Roxy. "I understand you're the one they refer to as Lady Gunsmith?"

"My name is Roxy Doyle, Judge."

"And what is your part in all this?"

"Apparently, whoever had her father killed also arranged to have her bushwhacked outside of town yesterday," Roxy said. "I kept that from happening."

"Why?" Tyler asked. "What was your reason for getting involved?"

"I don't like five-to-one odds," she said.

"And do you know who bushwhacked you?" Tyler asked Angie.

"We saw two of the men in a saloon last night," Angie said.

"Ah yes," Tyler said, "I heard there was a shooting. Are you sure they were two of the bushwhackers?"

"Well—" Angie started, but Roxy spoke up.

"Yes, we are."

"I see. Have you told the sheriff?"

"The sheriff has his hands full with the hanging," Roxy said. "I think we can take care of this ourselves."

"And by that do you mean you intend to kill someone?"

"If I was going to kill someone, I could've done it last night, when the idiot drew down on me."

"But you simply wounded and disarmed him."

"That's right."

"And what are your plans for Mr. Edward Sughrue?"

"If he tries to stop the hanging," Roxy said, "I'll stop him."

"And you believe he's going to do that?" Tyler asked. "To this point he has been seeking legal avenues to stop it, but to no avail. You believe he intends to use illegal means?"

"He's already tried to have Angie bushwhacked," Roxy said.

"Allegedly."

"And he's had a man named Kirk come and talk to us," Roxy went on.

Tyler made a face.

"I know Mr. Kirk. Did he threaten you?"

"No," Angie said, "he was a perfect gentleman, and bought us a drink."

"The threat," Roxy said, "was implied."

"Both of you ladies sound fairly educated," Tyler said, sitting back in his chair. "I'm impressed."

"I went to school," Angie said.

"I've been on my own since I was fifteen," Roxy said. "But I pay attention."

"I see." He folded his hands in his lap. "I'm afraid I don't see the purpose of this visit. Is this to warn me of what might occur?"

"This is to introduce myself," Angie said. "Nothing more. I don't expect anything of you."

"Except to attend the hanging," Roxy added.

"Oh, I'll be there," Judge Tyler said. "That's my job, to see my sentence through. If there's any attempt to keep it from happening, I expect the sheriff and his deputies to do their jobs."

"And we'll let them" Roxy said. "I'll only take a hand if someone tries to hurt Angie."

"And I'll defend myself," Angie added.

"You're certainly entitled to do so," Judge Tyler said to Angie. "Miss Doyle, it occurs to me that you might volunteer yourself to the sheriff as a temporary deputy."

"I don't think so, Judge," Roxy said. "I'm not the badge-toting kind. I don't like the rules. I need to be able to do what I have to do."

"Understood," Tyler said. "Well, then, I thank you both for coming in."

The two ladies had never taken a seat, so they simply turned and headed for the door.

"One other thing," Tyler called out.

They both turned.

"What's that?" Roxy asked.

"I don't like having gunfighters in my town," the Judge said.

"Are you telling me to leave?" Roxy asked.

"I'm telling you if it comes down to you and Mr. Kirk, I wouldn't be upset if you killed him," Tyler said. "But yes, then I'd want you to leave."

He turned his attention to something on his desk, and they left.

Chapter Sixteen

Roxy and Angie stopped just outside the City Hall door.

"I think you just got permission to kill Kirk," Angie said.

"I didn't need permission," Roxy said. "If he throws down on me, it'll happen."

"And then we'd have to leave town," Angie said, "which we'd be doing, anyway."

"So what's next?" Roxy asked.

"All we've got to do is be at the sheriff's office tomorrow to walk the prisoner to the gallows."

"So we've got the rest of the day to ourselves?" Roxy asked.

"Looks like it."

"How about a bath?" Roxy asked.

Angie stared at her.

***

The hotel had two bathtubs available for their guests, each in a separate room, which suited both Roxy and Angie. They weren't looking to bathe in the same room.

As they entered the lobby to arrange for the baths, Kirk was in a doorway across the street, watching. He waited, giving the women time to get to their rooms, then crossed the street and entered the lobby.

The desk clerk saw him approaching, recognized him and immediately began to perspire.

"Y-yes, sir?"

"The two women who just came in," Kirk said. "Are they in their rooms?"

"N-no, sir."

"Where are they, then?"

"They're taking baths, sir."

Kirk found the prospect of seeing either woman in a bathtub interesting.

"Where are the tubs?"

"Um, the end of the hall behind me, sir."

"The same room?"

"No, sir," the clerk said, "two separate rooms."

"Huh," Kirk said. It would have been even more interesting to see both women in the same room—or the same tub. Kirk had once been with two whores at the same time. It was a fond memory.

Kirk started down the hall.

"Um, sir, you can't go back there," the clerk said, but he said it so low and under his breath that Kirk didn't hear him.

***

Roxy got undressed, pulled a chair over by the tub so she could hang her gunbelt on the back of it. She also advised Angie to keep her rifle close.

"Maybe we should stand watch for each other," Angie suggested, "maybe even watch each other bathe?"

"Just keep your gun close," Roxy said, and went into her own room. She liked Angie, but watching each other bathe wasn't an option for her.

The water was hot and felt good soaking into her skin. She soaped up a cloth and began to wash her legs and thighs. When she got the cloth down between her legs, she again became aware of how long it had been since she'd been with a man. She closed her eyes and made sure she cleaned the area thoroughly. She had her eyes closed, but when she heard the door, she snapped them open and started to reach for her gun, even though she suspected it might be Angie.

"Take it easy," Kirk said, showing Roxy his two empty hands.

"You almost got your head blown off," Roxy told him. "What're you doing here?"

"I came to see you." Kirk closed the door behind him, then leaned back against it.

Roxy still had one leg in the air, and said, "Well, you're seeing me, all right."

"And it's a mighty pretty sight, I've got to say," Kirk commented. "That bath looks real inviting."

She went back to rubbing her leg and thigh, this time languidly.

"Well?" she said. "Do I have to invite you?"

He unstrapped his gun, giving her just a twinge that he might draw it, but instead he removed the belt.

"You mind if I set this nearby?" he asked.

"Use my chair," she said.

He did, setting the gunbelt down next to her, then standing next to the tub he started to undress. When his cock came into view, already rising to attention, she reached out and stroked it appreciatively.

"You better get in here before the water gets cold," she said. "Or I do."

He looked down at her naked body, those full breasts and hips, lovely skin with scattered freckles, and said, "I doubt that's gonna happen."

Chapter Seventeen

He slipped into the tub and sat facing her, his legs stretched out on either side. He was a well-built man without an ounce of fat, and his now fully hard cock rode up out of the water. She reached over to take it in her hand and stroke. He reached out with both hands for her breasts.

"I've never seen anything so beautiful," he said, using his thumbs to rub her nipples.

"You're kind of pretty yourself," she said, using her thumb to rub the head of his penis.

They moved toward each other and came together in a feverish kiss.

"We're gonna get a lot of this water on the floor," he said to her. "Maybe we should take this to your room."

"Oh no," Roxy said, "I've been waiting too long as it is."

"Really?" he said. "Since we met?"

"Much longer than that," she said. "You just sit still and let me do all the work."

"Whatayou—oh."

She slid into his lap, reached down to hold his cock in place, and slid down on it. Her pussy was wet from more than just the bath, and her heat closed around him, shutting him up, except for a groan.

She began to ride up and down on his stiff cock, closing her eyes and letting her head loll back. Yes, this was just what she needed. All she wanted from this point on was for Kirk to keep quiet, except for his grunts every time she came down on him. She also didn't want to make so much noise that Angie heard them in the next room. She might come and check to see what was going on. And it probably wouldn't make her happy, since she thought Kirk was so desirable.

Roxy laced her fingers behind his neck and started raising herself even higher before coming down. Each time they sloshed some water to the floor. But she didn't care if the tub ended up empty, as long as she got what she wanted.

"How about we—" he started, but she silenced him, first with a kiss, then a finger on his lips.

"Just keep quiet a little while longer," she said.

She knew there was always the chance he would reach over and grab his gun but wasn't as deep in the throes of passion as she seemed. She'd be able to feel the muscles in his body moving in a different way. And she thought she had him right where she wanted him, and before long, she had to muffle him again with her mouth as he exploded inside of her . . .

***

They got out of the tub moments later and started to dry off. The water—what was left of it—had gone tepid.

"How about we get dressed and take this up to your room?" Kirk asked.

"I don't think so, Mr. Kirk," she said. "I think I got what I needed, and there's always the possibility we're going to face each other over our guns."

"Now wait—are you going to tell me you could sleep with me and then kill me with no emotion?"

"Well—"

"Why did you even let me in here in the first place?" he asked.

Annoyed, Kirk grabbed his gunbelt and strapped it on. Roxy did the same.

"Sex has nothing to do with what you and me just did," she snapped.

"So we could have some fun, and then shoot each other, huh?" he asked.

"If it came to that," she said. "If one of us is gonna die, why not have some fun first?"

"You're an odd creature," he said. "Most women couldn't do what we just did, and not feel something."

"You mean like a man does?"

"Exactly," he said. "So you not only shoot like a man, you fuck like one, too."

"I think you're wrong, Kirk."

"About what?"

"Lots of women can have sex for fun," she said, "or for business, and not feel anything beyond the act."

"So I was just a piece of meat to you?"

"You're a lot more than that, Kirk," Roxy said, "which is why what we did won't go any further than this. There's just too much else going on."

"Like a hanging."

"Exactly."

"Maybe there won't be a hanging," Kirk said.

"I guess we'll just have to see about that," Roxy said, "won't we?"

Chapter Eighteen

Kirk left, and Roxy gave him time to get out of the hotel before stepping into the hall herself and knocking on the door of the room where Angie was bathing.

"Are you done?" she called out.

"Not quite," Angie called back. "Why don't you wait in your room?"

"I'll be in the lobby," Roxy told her. "Take your time."

She thought she heard Angie laugh, and then she called out, "All right."

When Roxy got to the lobby, she noticed the young clerk was not behind the desk. She went over and sat on a lobby divan that was against the wall.

***

In Angie's tub, the blonde was riding up and down on the hard cock of the skinny, young desk clerk. He had knocked on her door earlier, and she had simply called, "Come in."

He opened the door and entered, then his eyes went wide when he saw Angie's pale skin and large breasts in the tub.

"Can I help you?" she asked him, amused by the look on his face.

"Ma'am," he said, staring as she soaped her brown-nippled breasts, "I just wanted to warn you, uh, Mr. Kirk was askin' about you and your, uh, friend."

"Really? When was this?"

"Just a few minutes ago."

"And where is he now?"

"Uh, he walked back here, but I guess he, uh—"

"So he's next door, with Miss Doyle?" she asked.

"I guess so."

"That bitch," Angie said, but there was no rancor in her tone.

"Ma'am?"

She looked at him, then at his trousers. He wasn't a bad looking young man, and if Roxy was satisfying her urges, why shouldn't she?

"When's the last time you had a bath?"

"Ma'am?"

"Never mind," she said, "take off your pants."

"My . . . pants?"

"Well, you can't very well get into the tub and fuck me with your pants on, can you?"

79

***

"When the clerk came back out to the desk Roxy noticed his hair was wet. Also, when he looked over at Roxy, he blushed.

She stood up and walked toward him.

"What's your name?"

"Um, Dennis."

"Dennis, are you the one who let Mr. Kirk into the back?" she asked.

"Ma'am, I couldn't stop him—"

"But you warned Miss Blackthorne he was here, right?" Roxy asked.

"Uh, yes, ma'am, but that's because I thought he was already, uh, in your room—"

"Yes, yes, no problem," she said. "But you didn't see him leave, right?"

"No, Ma'am," he said, "I wasn't, uh, out here—"

"Relax, Dennis," Roxy said. "I'm not going to tell your boss you took the time for an afternoon bath."

"Oh, uh, yeah," he said, "thanks, Miss Doyle."

"Is Angie coming out?" she asked.

"Um, yeah, she was, uh, dryin' off—"

She hadn't let him finish a sentence yet, so she said, "Okay, just relax, Dennis. Thanks."

"Yes, Ma'am."

Roxy walked back to the divan. She was still sitting there when Angie came out, her hair also wet. She spotted Roxy and came walking over, a spring in her step.

"You little tart," she said, sitting next to her with a smile.

"Okay, so I thought he might be there to shoot me, but instead we ended up in the tub together," Roxy said. "I tried to keep it quiet. But Dennis told you, didn't he?"

"Dennis?"

"The desk clerk?"

"Oh, yeah," Angie said, smiling, "Dennis. What a nice young man."

"Until you corrupted him."

"Hey, he came in, he saw me naked, stepped on his tongue, so I invited him in. Besides, you were a little busy right next door."

"Yeah," Roxy said, "that might've been a mistake."

"Didn't you enjoy it?"

"Well, yeah, while we were doing it," Roxy said. "I didn't enjoy what came after."

She explained to Angie about the conversation she had with Kirk.

"So you fucked him, and then rejected him?"

"Yes."

"I'll bet he didn't take that well," Angie said.

"Well, you didn't form a relationship with skinny Dennis, over there, did you?"

"Jesus, no . . . although he does have a pretty nice tallywacker. So young . . ."

Chapter Nineteen

"What's on your mind?" Edward Sughrue asked Kirk.

Kirk, sitting across the desk from Sughrue, said, "I think if I take Lady Gunsmith today, the other one will be easier to get rid of."

"Talk plain," Sughrue said, "you're talking about killing both women?"

"I'm talking about killing Roxy Doyle," Kirk said. "Then you can have the other one killed. I mean, that's what you tried yesterday, right?"

Sughrue didn't answer right away, and when he did, he sounded unsure.

"I'm thinking about just breaking the boy out tonight," he admitted.

"You told me you didn't want him to be on the run," Kirk reminded his boss. "If I kill Doyle fair and square, nobody's on the run. And if you successfully bushwhack the Blackthorne woman, same thing."

"When would you do this?"

"Before dark," Kirk said. "Then you could have Blackthorne taken care of after dark. By morning there'll be nobody to hang Jerry. You'll have time to make up your mind about what you really wanna do."

Sughrue thought again, then asked, "How much?"

"Double."

"What?"

"It's Lady Gunsmith," Kirk pointed out.

"Which means you get a bigger reputation when you kill her," Sughrue said.

"It also means there's a chance she'll kill me," Kirk said. "You don't have to pay me until after."

"You really think she has a chance against you?"

"No," Kirk said, as if it was a stupid question. "She's a woman!"

"A beautiful woman," Sughrue said. "You've no qualms about doing it?"

"Not one," Kirk said.

"All right, then," Sughrue said. "Let me know when it's done."

"I won't have to," Kirk said, standing up. "It'll be all over town. You'll hear about it."

"Kirk!" Sughrue said, as the gunman reached the door.

"Yeah?"

"Get it done, man," Sughrue said.

"That's what you're paying me for."

***

"What do you think?" Angie asked, as they came out of the hotel.

"I think if Kirk can kill me today, you'll be easy pickings."

"If they bushwhack me again," Angie said. "If they come right at me, I can take care of myself."

"Not if there's five of them, again," Roxy said.

"So what do you want to do?" Angie asked. "Call out Kirk?"

"I don't think I'll have to," Roxy said. "His ego was pretty bruised when he left here. He just has to make sure he's going to get paid to do it."

"By Sughrue, you mean."

"Who else?"

"What if we go after him?" Angie asked.

"You mean kill Sughrue?"

"Not necessarily," Angie said. "Scare him, maybe."

"We can go see him," Roxy said. "But I don't know if he'll scare or not. He's probably already scared that he's going to lose his son."

"You think he'd risk a blood bath to save him?"

85

"I don't have children," Roxy said, "and I don't think I have any maternal instinct, so I don't know what somebody would do to save their child."

"I'm willing to cause a blood bath to avenge my father," Angie pointed out. "Wouldn't you?"

"I'm still looking for my father," Roxy said. "After all these years, I don't even know if I'll like him."

"I don't think you ever told me his name," Angie said. "Or maybe I just never asked."

"He's Gavin Doyle."

"Wait," Angie said, "I know that name. The bounty hunter?"

"That's him," Roxy said. "Left me with a family when I was very young. They abused me, and I went out on my own when I was fifteen."

"Wow, you poor kid."

"I'm okay with it," Roxy said. "I took my life into my own hands."

"And became Lady Gunsmith?"

"That came from a chance meeting with Clint Adams," Roxy said. "He took me under his wing, we got into a firefight together, and since then the name stuck. So I need you to tell me, do you think Sughrue would do *anything* to save his son?"

"I believe he would," Angie said.

"Then there isn't much chance we'd be able to scare him out of it, is there?"

Chapter Twenty

Since they had already talked with the judge, taken baths, had sex and decided there was no point in talking to Edward Sughrue, Roxy and Angie decided not to hide in their rooms. They picked a small saloon to have a couple of beers and wait for suppertime to arrive.

They took their drinks to a table in the half-filled saloon. There were no girls working the floor, just a burly bartender mopping the bar with a dirty rag, and a few other customers, who were giving them the eye.

"You know," Angie said, "I'll bet you and me could have a lot of fun if I wasn't so intent on avenging my father's murder."

"I'm not about to try to talk you out of it," Roxy said, "but yeah, I bet we could."

"The word's probably gotten around about who we are, so these fellas aren't staring at us because we're pretty."

"Even though we are."

"Right."

They both laughed.

They sipped their beers, drinking slowly.

"I think I like it better thinking their afraid of us," Angie said.

"I don't think we've got any bushwhackers in here," Roxy said. "We might find them in a bigger saloon."

"Then maybe we should be drinking in bigger saloons," Angie said.

"That's what I was thinking," Roxy said. "And let's find the best restaurant in town for supper."

"If they want to come after us, we'll be out there."

"Can you handle a pistol?" Roxy asked.

"I'd shoot myself in the foot," Angie said. "I'm just a little better with a rifle. Sorry."

"Don't apologize," Roxy said. "We'll be at closer range than we were yesterday."

"If we encounter Kirk, you want me to leave him to you?" Angie asked.

"Yes," Roxy said, "I'll just need you to watch my back. He might decide to bring some help."

"You can count on me," Angie said. "After all, you been watching my back all this time."

"And I'll walk with you tomorrow morning to get the kid up those steps," Roxy said.

"Hopefully, by then we'll also know who killed my dad. Then we can get out of town."

But Roxy knew Angie didn't only want to know who killed her dad, she wanted her revenge, as well. And they weren't going to leave Copper City until that happened.

***

They went to one more saloon, a larger one, drank more beer, then walked the street until they found a large restaurant that looked to be doing a brisk supper rush. It was called O'GRADY'S STEAKHOUSE.

"This looks like the place," Roxy said.

Angie looked in the window.

"Appears like everything from businessmen to families," she observed.

"And you and me," Roxy said. "Come on."

As they entered, a man in a tuxedo met them just inside the door.

"Ladies," he asked, "are you, uh, meeting someone?"

"No," Roxy said, "it's just us."

"Of course," he said. "This way. A table by the window?"

"No," Roxy said, "away from the window."

"Of course. Follow me, please."

As they walked across the floor and drew attention, Angie whispered, "I think we're underdressed."

"Hey," Roxy said, "we're clean."

They sat at their table and were assured that a waiter would be with them shortly. It didn't even take that long as a small, fat, white-haired man wearing a white shirt and black apron came over.

"What can I get for you ladies?"

"Well," Roxy said, "this *is* a steakhouse, so I'll have a steak."

"I will, too."

"We make them rare, unless you want it some other way," the waiter said.

"Rare's fine," Roxy said.

"I'll have the same."

"And we'll have two beers," Roxy said.

"Comin' up, ladies."

"Before you, go," Roxy said. "are there any important people here?"

"Important?"

"You know, like the city manager, or one of the town council? Someone who has pull in town?"

"Well," the waiter said, looking around, "there are several businessmen, some of them sit on the council, but the mayor's not here. And some are ranchers here with their families."

"All right, thanks," Roxy said.

"You didn't ask him if there were any bushwhackers here," Angie pointed out, and they both laughed.

Chapter Twenty-One

Their meal was uneventful and fulfilled their intention of showing they weren't afraid to move about.

But when they came out of the steakhouse, they noticed the street was quiet and deserted.

"This isn't good," Roxy said.

"What's going on?" Angie asked.

"If I'm right," Roxy said, "Kirk's about to make his play. The question is, will he make it alone?"

***

Word had filtered throughout town that the hang "lady" and Lady Gunsmith were in O'Grady's Steakhouse. That was all Kirk needed to hear. He went over and took up his position right across the street.

People walking by recognized Kirk, knew who and what he was. So the gossip now began to spread that something was in the air on Main Street. Folks got behind closed doors and stayed there, peering out.

***

Judge Tyler got the word from his clerk.

"How do you know this, Jason?" he asked.

"It's all over town, Judge," the young man said. "The two women are in the O'Grady's, and Kirk's right across the street."

"And is he alone?"

"Well . . . he looks like he's alone," the clerk admitted.

"All right, thank you for letting me know," Judge Tyler said.

"Uh, sir, could I have the next hour off?"

"For what purpose?"

"I wanna watch them," Jason admitted.

"You get back to work or I'll fire your ass!" the judge snapped.

"Yessir!"

As the clerk left, the judge leaned back in his chair, and waited . . .

***

Sughrue got the word from Vance Hackett, who came into his office, short of breath.

"What the hell, were you running?" Sughrue asked.

"Yes, sir," Vance said, "It's gonna happen now."

"What is?"

"Kirk, and Lady Gunsmith," Vance said. "They're gonna face off."

"Where?"

"Main Street."

"When?"

"Now, sir!" Vance said. "Doyle and Angie Blackthorne are in O'Grady's. Kirk's waitin' outside."

"Where's the sheriff?"

"Ain't seen 'im."

"Well, get over to his office and make sure he doesn't interfere."

"But I wanted to watch!"

"Never mind," Sughrue snapped at him. "Just do what I tell you."

Vance headed for the door, then turned.

"Ain't you gonna go watch?"

"No, I'm not," Sughrue said. "But you be sure to let me know the outcome as soon as it's over."

"How will I know that?" Vance asked. "I ain't gettin' to watch."

"When it's over," Sughrue said, "somebody will come for the sheriff. You'll be with him."

"Ah, right," Vance said.

"When they call for him, you go along. Then you'll let me know what happened."

"Right."

Vance left Sughrue's office. The man sat back in his chair, wondering if he'd hear the shots?

***

"There he is," Roxy said, "across the street."

"He's not moving," Angie said.

"He will."

"Where do you want me?" Angie asked.

"Just move to one side, and keep your eye on the windows and rooftops," Roxy said. "If he's got help, it'll be somebody with a rifle. All you have to do is get them before they get me."

Angie flexed her hands on her rifle.

"I'll try," she promised.

"At the very least you can make them take cover," Roxy said. "I just need to be able to concentrate on Kirk."

"And here he comes," Angie said.

Roxy looked across the street and saw that Kirk had stepped off the boardwalk and started across.

"All right," Roxy said, "here we go."

Chapter Twenty-Two

Roxy stepped down into the street. She gave the windows and rooftops across the street a quick check but saw nothing. After that, she'd have to leave it to Angie. As for the windows and rooftops behind her, she didn't step into the street far enough for anyone to have an angle on her.

"Do you really want to do this now?" Roxy asked Kirk.

"I don't have much of a choice, Miss Doyle," he said. "It's getting dark, and it has to be done before tomorrow."

"That's what Sughrue told you?"

"Never mind who told me what." He looked past her at Angie. "She gonna take a hand?"

"Only if you've got help," Roxy said.

He laughed.

"Why would I need help?" he asked. "You're a woman."

Some brave people had gathered up and down the street, waiting and watching. Others were still inside, peering out their windows and doors.

"Where is Mr. Sughrue, anyway?" Roxy asked. "Isn't he going to watch?"

"I don't know where he is or what he's doin'," Kirk said. "And I don't care. You know, you should've been nicer to me."

"Is that what this is about, Kirk?" Roxy asked. "I hurt your feelings?"

"Lady Gunsmith," he said, shaking his head. "That's a hard name to live up to, ain't it? Tell me, if I kill you, is he gonna come after me? Clint Adams?"

"I don't know," Roxy said. "But I don't think you're going to find out."

"You think you're faster than me? Is that it?"

"No," she said, "I know I am."

Kirk laughed, but it sounded like a bark.

"And how do you know that?"

"Because you're talking too much, Kirk," Roxy said. "If you thought you were faster, you would've drawn by now. You're trying to distract me with talk."

"I'm through talkin'," Kirk growled.

"It's about time," Roxy said, watching his eyes, his shoulders. Some men you could see it in their eyes when they were going to draw, others gave it away with their shoulders. The good ones—well, you just had to beat them. There was no tell.

For Kirk, it was his eyes. Still, he turned out to be pretty fast. He almost overcame that tell, that slight flick of his eyes the moment before he drew.

He had his gun half out of his holster when Roxy drew and shot him dead center, just the way Clint Adams had taught her. When you didn't have time to play, you had to hit them dead center.

Kirk staggered a few feet back, then rather than falling forward onto his face, or backward onto his back, his knees simply buckled, and he collapsed, almost in sections.

Angie quickly stepped into the street, her rifle ready, but there were no shots.

"He was alone," she said.

"He was a fool," Roxy said.

She walked to his body, leaned over, checked to be sure he was dead. Then she straightened up, replaced the spent shell with a live round, and holstered her gun.

"What now?" Angie asked.

"We wait," Roxy said. "The sheriff should be along."

People began to come out onto the street from their various vantage points. Those who were already outside watching moved closer, others came from behind closed doors, still more spilled out of a saloon and the steakhouse. They were all amazed by the speed of Roxy Doyle's draw.

And then the sheriff appeared, followed by a man Roxy recognized. He had been in the saloon the night before, when she shot the kid called Darius.

As the sheriff approached her, the other fella's eyes widened, and then he turned and ran. He was going to report to his boss, Sughrue. That was one man who was going to be disappointed.

"What happened here?" Sheriff Homer asked.

"I think you know," Roxy said. "He called me out, just like everybody knew he would."

"Is he dead?"

"Stone cold," Roxy said.

"I'll get some men to move the body," Homer said. "I'll need you to come to my office to make a statement."

"Why?" she asked. "You've got plenty of witnesses, plus you *knew* this was going to happen. There's no doubt it was a fair fight."

"Still—"

"I'm not coming to your office, Sheriff," Roxy said. "There's no need."

"Where will you be?" Homer asked.

"A saloon, my hotel, who knows?" Roxy asked. "But I'll tell you where I'll be tomorrow morning? At your office, to collect the prisoner for hanging." She looked at Angie. "We'll both be there."

They turned and walked away.

Chapter Twenty-Three

Roxy and Angie were going to go to the Ace Queen Saloon, but instead they stopped in at The Hellion. They each got a beer from the bartender, and then went to a table. The word had already gone around that Lady Gunsmith had killed Kirk, and nobody got in their way.

"You've earned a lot of respect."

"Respect, fear," Roxy said. "That's not the way I want to earn either one."

"So what do we do now?" Angie asked.

"We keep you alive to hang Jerry Sughrue," Roxy said. "First thing in the morning."

***

"She killed him," Vance told Sughrue. "From what I heard, easy as you please."

"Kirk was fast," Sughrue said.

"Well, she was faster," Vance said. "All the witnesses that I talked to said they never saw her draw."

"Goddamnit!" Sughrue snapped.

"So I guess Jerry's gonna hang tomorrow," Vance said.

"Not if I have anything to say about it. How many men do you have?"

"Well, Darius has a busted arm, so there's four of us—" Vance started.

"Can you get more?"

"Well, sure—"

"Will they all be idiots?" Sughrue asked. "Find a few men who have an ounce of brain?"

"I'll do that," Vance said, "but you'll have to pay them more."

"I'll pay them whatever it takes to keep Jerry from hanging," Sughrue said.

"All right, then." Vance stood, then turned. "You're not gonna want anybody to go up against Lady Gunsmith, are ya?"

"Not alone," Sughrue said. "I thought Kirk had a brain, but that was an idiotic thing to do. You get those men and come to my house tonight at eight."

"All of us?"

"Yes, all of you!"

"Yes, sir."

As Vance left, Sughrue sat back. He didn't know yet what he was going to do with all these men, but if they comprised a small army, he'd be happy just to let them loose.

***

It was Sheriff Homer who brought the news to Judge Tyler.

"Shot dead in the street, slick as you please," Homer said, standing in front of the judge's desk.

"Is that a surprise?" Tyler asked.

"Judging by her reputation, no," Homer said, "but she's still a woman, and Kirk was fast."

"And now he's dead," the judge said. "Where is she now?"

"I don't know," the lawman said. "A saloon, her hotel . . ."

"Did you take her to your office for a statement?"

"She refused," Homer said. "Said everybody saw it, everybody knows it was a fair fight."

The judge stared at the man.

"I couldn't *force* 'er!" Homer complained.

"What if I told you to run her out of town?" Tyler asked him.

"I guess I'd have to give up my badge, Judge," Homer admitted. "I can't go against her."

Judge Tyler didn't reply.

"Do you want my badge, Judge?" Homer asked.

"No," Tyler said, "not with the hanging coming in the morning. Are your deputies ready?"

"They are."

"Let's just hope it goes off without a hitch," Tyler said. "But Sughrue's still got all night to pull something."

"He ain't gonna get it done legally, is he?"

"Not a chance," Tyler said.

"So you think he'll try something before mornin'?"

"He's got to," the judge said.

"Maybe I should get a few more deputies."

"Do you know anyone who'll take on the badge?"

"To hang Jerry Sughrue? I'm lucky I have the two that I have," Homer said.

"All right, then, just make do with what you got."

"Yessir."

"I'll see you in the morning, Sheriff," the judge said. "That's all."

"Yessir."

As Homer left, the judge stood and walked to his window which overlooked Main Street. From there he could see the front of the sheriff's office, but not the gallows in the back. It was just as well. He'd get all he could stand of that structure in the morning.

Chapter Twenty-Four

Roxy and Angie had one beer in The Hellion Saloon, then left. No one approached them, and few even looked at them.

Outside it was getting dark, and they decided to just go back to the hotel.

Dennis, the young clerk, was on duty, and immediately blushed and looked away.

"I'm really not that sleepy," Angie said. "Do you want to bring a deck of cards to my room?"

"You can take Dennis up to your room and have him tire you out," Roxy suggested.

"I don't think so," Angie said. "I just needed the release, but I don't need him to get clingy."

"I know what you mean," Roxy said. "Okay, we can play some poker."

"Good! I'd rather do that than sit in my room alone."

"And we might as well stay together," Roxy said. "If Sughrue's going to try anything else, it'll have to be tonight."

"Maybe we can get Dennis to bring up a pot of coffee," Angie suggested.

"I'll ask him," Roxy said. "That way you don't have to deal with him, again."

"I'll meet you upstairs."

Angie trotted up the steps while Roxy went to the front desk.

"Dennis, do you have a deck of cards?"

"Yes, Ma'am," he said. "I always keep 'em here for guests." He reached under the desk and handed her a sealed deck.

"And could you have someone bring a pot of coffee and two cups up to Miss Blackthorne's room?"

"Yes, Ma'am. Anythin' else?"

"No, that's it," Roxy said. "Thanks."

She went up to Angie's room. The door had been left ajar for her. She entered, saw Angie seated on the bed.

"Stud or draw?" she asked, brandishing the deck.

"Draw, I suppose." Angie said. "I'm not very good at either."

"You know, since we've met you've told me you're not a good shot and not a good poker player. What are you good at, Angie?"

"Not much of anything, I guess," she said.

"What were you doing before you decided to . . . to take up where your father left off?"

"I was back East, going to parties and dinners. I was bored so I came out West to be with him, only he was killed. So now we're going to find out if I'm a good hangman."

"How many times did you watch your father do it?" Roxy asked.

"Once," Angie said, "but he talked about it a lot when I was smaller."

"To a kid?"

"To others, but I listened," Angie said. "I always listened."

The coffee was delivered to the door by a waiter. There was a large pot, two cups, a small pitcher of cream, and a bowl of sugar cubes. There were so many sugar cubes, that they decided that was what they'd play poker for.

Roxy dealt and they started. They were soon laughing out loud because they realized neither one of them was a good poker player.

At one point, while Angie shuffled and dealt, Roxy stood up and walked to the window. Angie's room overlooked Main Street, which she didn't like. At the moment, the street was dark and empty.

"We have to move to my room," she said.

"Why?"

"It overlooks the alley. Nobody can get a shot through the window, and there's no access from outside.

Besides, the waiter delivered the coffee here, so some-body knows which room we're in."

"Okay, let's move after this hand," Angie said, look-ing at her cards.

"Oh, you got a good hand?"

"You'll see."

Roxy came back, sat on the bed and picked up her cards.

"What do you do?"

"Two cubes," Roxy said, since she had three threes.

"I call," Angie said, "and raise you five."

"Well, well," Roxy said. "I call."

"How many cards?" Angie asked.

"Two."

"Dealer takes two."

They both looked at their cards.

"What do you do?" Angie asked.

"I'll check to you, since you raised."

"Five sugar cubes," Angie said.

"I've only got two left," Roxy pointed out.

Angie held her cards close to her chest.

"What else you got?"

"You mean . . . money?"

"Not necessarily," Angie said. "How about . . . if I win, you have to carry the tray of coffee to your room."

"And if I win, you do?" Roxy asked.

"Right."

"Then I call," Roxy said. "What do you have?"

"Full house," Angie said, "tens full of kings." She set the cards down in a spread.

"Too bad," Roxy said, setting her cards down, "four threes." She stood up. "I'll carry your rifle. Let's move."

Chapter Twenty-Five

Roxy opened the door and allowed Angie to go out ahead of her carrying the tray of coffee, cream and sugar cubes. The tray was heavy, made of silver, and took two hands to carry. The minute Angie stepped out, her eyes widened, and she said, "Holy shit!"

Gunfire erupted in the hall . . .

***

Earlier that night, Vance arrived at Sughrue's house with six men.

"This all you got?" Sughrue asked, as he opened the door.

Vance leaned in.

"You said you wanted men with half a brain," he said.

"Can they shoot?"

"They can do that, yeah," Vance said.

"Okay, come on in and I'll tell you all what's expected of you."

***

What was expected of them was to get into the hotel without a fuss and go to the second floor. But when they entered the lobby, Dennis, the desk clerk, looked at them and frowned.

"What're all you fellas doin' in here?" he asked.

"What's your name?" Vance asked.

"Uh, Dennis."

"Well Dennis," Vance said, "take a walk and come back in half an hour or so."

"I, uh, can't leave the desk for that long," Dennis said.

"You can leave the desk," Vance said, "or die behind it. Your choice."

Dennis left the desk in a hurry.

"All right, boys," Vance said. "Let's take a look."

He got the register and checked to see what rooms Roxy Doyle and Angela Blackthorne were in.

"Down the hall from each other," he said. "Let's go."

The five men followed Vance up the steps . . .

***

Roxy heard several bullets strike the silver tray, saving Angie's life. Then she grabbed Angie's arm and yanked her back into the room.

"Are you hit?" she asked.

"I don't think so," Angie said. "I—I got the tray up in front of me."

"Here," Roxy said, shoving the rifle into Angie's hand. "They're stacked up in the hall. Just keep firing. Ready?"

"I'm ready."

Roxy and Angie stepped into the hall together and started firing . . .

***

The men were expecting that Angie was dead, figuring they only had Roxy to worry about. Six against one seemed good odds to them, but when Roxy and Angie stepped out and started firing, they were surprised.

Vance was still in front, so the first bullets struck him and took him down. After that, the bullets made wet slapping sounds as the other men fell victim to a hail of lead. By the time they began to return fire, there were only half of them left, and they were no match for the two women.

In moments, the hall was filled with dead . . .

***

When Dennis, the desk clerk, had left the hotel, he ran directly to the sheriff's office.

"There's half a dozen men at the hotel, Sheriff, gonna kill them two ladies."

"Whataya expect me to do about it?" Homer asked. "I'm one man."

"You got deputies!" Dennis snapped.

"Not til tomorrow mornin', for the hangin'," Homer said. "I ain't goin' against six men. Besides, them two women can handle it."

"You ain't gonna do nothin'?"

At that moment they could both hear the shots from the hotel.

"I'm gonna wait until the shooting stops," Homer said.

***

As doors opened and people peered out, Roxy yelled, "Back inside, folks! It's all over."

She and Angie walked down the hall as doors slammed and checked all the men.

"They're all dead," Roxy said.

Angie went back to the room, returned with the silver tray. She showed Roxy the dents the bullets had made in it.

"Lucky I had a shield," Angie said.

"Lucky you thought to hold it up," Roxy said. "Are you hit at all?"

Angie looked down, patted herself, and said, "Don't seem to be."

At that moment, they heard somebody running up the steps, pointed their guns, but relaxed when they saw Sheriff Homer.

"What's goin' on?" he demanded.

"Right on time, Sheriff," Roxy said. "It's all over."

Chapter Twenty-Six

With six dead men piled up like cordwood in the hall, Roxy agreed to go over to the sheriff's office, along with Angie. She figured in the time it took her to get that done, the bodies would be cleared away.

She and Angie made out their statements and signed them, pushed them across to the sheriff's side of the desk.

"Thank you, ladies."

"Tell me, Sheriff," Roxy said, "did you recognize any of those dead men? Do they work for Edward Sughrue?"

"I'd have to take a better look," Homer said, "maybe at the undertaker's."

"We recognize at least one of them as a bushwhacker," Angie said, "so I'm assuming this was Sughrue's final attempt to keep me from hanging his son."

"But you can't prove that," Homer pointed out.

"No, I can't," Angie said. "That doesn't mean I won't go find him and put a hole in him."

"Now, wait a minute—"

"Oh, don't worry, Sheriff," Roxy said. "We're not going to do that. After all he's done, we want Mr. Sughrue to watch Angie hang the boy tomorrow."

They both stood up.

"But if he does try to stop me in the morning," Angie added, "I *will* put a hole in him."

"If he tries to stop the hangin'," Homer said, "I'll have to put a hole in 'im!"

They left his office.

***

Sughrue got tired of waiting at home for word of what had happened, so he went for a walk. That was when he heard that all six men, including Vance, had been killed and were at the undertaker's.

He went back home, sat on his sofa with a gun in his hand, and waited for morning.

***

Roxy and Angie went back to their hotel, where Dennis gave them each a new room.

"Uh, I'm sorry I couldn't do anythin' when those men came in," he told Angie. "All I could think of was to go for the sheriff, but he was afraid to come over."

115

Angie was nice enough to lean forward, stroke the boy's cheek and say, "You did what you could, Dennis. Thanks."

He blushed as the women continued upstairs to their new rooms, which were across from each other.

They opened both their doors to inspect the interior. Even though they thought Edward Sughrue had used all his ammunition, they still wanted to be sure.

Roxy entered Angie's room with her, and the blonde asked, "Do you think Sughrue's done?"

"What else can he do?" Roxy asked. "Even if he wanted to send six more men after us, I doubt he'd find them in this town. And he doesn't have time to send for professionals. That's probably what he should've done in the first place, but apparently he actually spent time trying to do it legally."

"I just hope he doesn't do anything real stupid in the morning," Angie said. "It's bad enough he's got to watch his son die."

"You're not starting to feel bad for him, are you?" Roxy asked.

"No," she said, shaking her head, "he had something to do with killing my father. I don't want him dead, I want him alive and suffering."

"That's what I thought," Roxy said. "I'm going to turn in, unless you want to play more poker."

"No," Angie said, "I'm done. I want to get a good night's sleep and get up early enough to have breakfast before I hang Jerry Sughrue."

"Are you sure you want a heavy meal before you do that?" Roxy asked. "You've never done it before."

"I want everybody to see me alive and kicking, eating breakfast and then walking to the jail."

"All right, I get it," Roxy said. "And I'll be right there."

"You've been right there every step of the way, so far, Roxy," Angie said, "so I know you'll be there tomorrow. And I thank you."

Angie gave Roxy a long, tight hug which, to Roxy's way of thinking, became somewhat awkward. Then Angie broke the hug and stared into her face.

"I'll see you in the morning, my friend," she said.

"In the lobby," Roxy said, "for breakfast."

Angie nodded and stepped back.

Roxy went to her own room, and the two women closed their doors.

Chapter Twenty-Seven

Roxy rose the next morning, looked over at the chair she'd jammed underneath her doorknob. She got up, washed, dressed, and moved the chair. Then she strapped on her gun and went down to the lobby.

Dennis was behind the desk and returned her smile.

"Has Miss Blackthorne been down, yet?" she asked.

"No, Ma'am."

"I'll wait for her in the lobby, then."

She walked to a divan and sat. It was so early that no one else went through the lobby, either entering or leaving. Before long, Angie came walking down the stairs carrying her rifle and her rope. She said good morning to Dennis and joined Roxy on the divan.

"Ready to eat?" Roxy asked.

"Yes," Angie said, "but maybe not a very heavy breakfast."

"Starting to feel it?"

Angie nodded.

"Right in the pit of my stomach," Angie said.

"Not going to change your mind, are you?"

"Not a chance," Angie said.

"Good. Let's go to that café on Main Street. It'll be a short walk to the sheriff's office after."

They left the hotel and headed for the café. That early the streets were empty. Some of the stores were just opening their doors, shopkeepers were setting inventory out on the boardwalk, or simply sweeping. The few people outside stopped what they were doing, since they knew who the two women were and what was scheduled for that morning.

When they reached the café, they were able to choose whatever table they wanted and ordered breakfast. Roxy noticed Angie kept looking at the door.

"Are you expecting Sughrue?" she asked.

"Or somebody," she said. "One last ditch effort to save his boy."

"I think he's more likely to take one more run at the judge than at you," Roxy said, "but there's no harm in staying alert."

"The sheriff and his deputies must be scared stiff," Angie said. "Seems to me this town needs to put some new people in positions of authority."

"We won't see it," Roxy said. "Are you going to be ready to leave after the trap door opens?"

"I don't know," Angie said. "I might still want to take a run at getting Sughrue to admit he had my dad killed."

"Once his boy's dead, he just might admit it," Roxy said.

"We'll see."

When breakfast came, they started eating. Roxy had seen hangings before and didn't let them affect her appetite, so she had ham-and-eggs. She noticed Angie had only ordered some biscuits and was picking at those.

***

Judge Tyler was preparing to leave his office and walk to the sheriff's office when the door opened and Edward Sughrue walked in.

"If you intend to make one more plea, don't, Edward," Tyler said. "There's nothing I can do."

"Well, there may be something I can do, Judge," Sughrue said.

"Like what?"

Sughrue reached into his jacket and took out a small barreled Colt, which he pointed at the judge.

"Don't be a fool Edward—" Tyler started.

"If you had a son," Sughrue said, "you'd know that being a fool is all I have left, Judge. Come on, we're going to walk over to the sheriff's office together."

"You think you're going to trade your boy for me?"

"I guess we're going to find out. Move!"

***

Roxy paid the bill and met Angie out in front of the café, where Angie was fingering her rope and noose.

"Are you ready?" Roxy asked.

"As I'll ever be," she said. "First we'll set the rope, then go into the jail and get the prisoner."

By the time they reached the back of the jail, where the gallows was, a crowd had already gathered. They watched as Angie and Roxy ascended, attached the rope, made sure it was secure, then came back down.

"This outta be good," a man said, loudly, "watching a girl hang a man."

"A boy, you mean," someone else said.

"Ignore them," Roxy said.

They walked around the building to the front of the sheriff's office. As they entered, they saw sheriff Homer seated at his desk flanked by two young deputies.

"Is he ready?" Angie asked.

"He's ready," Homer said, standing up. He grabbed his keys from a wall peg and led the way into the cell block. The boy inside stood up and stared, his eyes watery. There was a tray nearby with his breakfast on it, hardly consumed.

"It's time, Jerry," Homer said.

"I can see all them people outside my window," Jerry said. "Guess they can't wait."

Homer opened the cell door.

"A hangin's always a spectacle," the lawman said. "Put your hands out."

Jerry extended his hands and the sheriff attached the chains to his wrists. Angie stepped up and checked to be sure they were secure.

"I'll take it from here, Sheriff," she said. "Your men can walk behind."

"Yes, Ma'am. What about the priest?"

"What?" Angie asked.

"There's a priest—"

"Oh, yeah, fine," Angie said. "He can stand up there with me."

The two young deputies were alternately looking at Roxy then Angie. Roxy because she was Lady Gunsmith, Angie because she was a lady hangman.

There was a back door that led right from the cell block. Angie led Jerry to it, standing on one side while Roxy stood on the other. This was not something Roxy had ever imagined she would be doing in her life.

Chapter Twenty-Eight

The crowd had been buzzing, but when the back door opened, they fell silent. Angie and Roxy stepped through, with Jerry Sughrue between them, wild-eyed and shaking. To his credit, however, although his eyes were watery, he had not broken down into tears.

Behind them the three lawmen came, holding their rifles. Angie had left her own rifle in the sheriff's office. She was satisfied with Roxy's gun at her side.

They walked Jerry to the bottom of the steps, where the lawmen spread out and the priest joined them. Roxy and Angie walked up the stairway with Jerry, positioning him on the trap door beneath the noose. Off to the side, the priest was reading from the bible.

When the prisoner was in place, Angie removed the shackles, and then tied the boy's hands behind his back.

"Do you want a hood, Jerry?" Angie asked.

"A h-hood?"

"Over your head so you can't see anything?"

"N-no, I don't want that," he said. "I don't l-like the dark."

"All right."

She slid the noose over his head, making sure it was tight, when they heard the voice call out. "That'll be far enough!"

Everyone turned to see who had spoken. Two more men came out the back door of the jail. Roxy saw Judge Tyler, with Edward Sughrue behind him, holding a gun.

"Let my boy go," Sughrue shouted, "or I'll kill the judge."

"If you kill the judge," Angie called back, "you might as well walk right up here and stand next to your boy, Mr. Sughrue."

"You bitch!" he snapped. "Let him go!"

"Not a chance," she said. "You had my father killed, and now you're going to watch your boy hang."

"I had to do something!" he shouted. "I'm sorry your father had to die, but—"

"That's just it," Angie said, cutting him off. "He didn't *have* to die. Killing the hangman accomplishes nothing. As you can see, somebody just comes along and takes his place."

"Look, we can argue this all day," Sughrue said. "Cut him loose or the judge dies."

"And you have to understand," Angie said, "I don't care. You can kill the judge. All I want is for you to see your boy hang. He's a murderer, he was sentenced, and he deserves it."

She stepped back, threw the lever that opened the trap door. It slammed open, and Jerry Sughrue fell through. Roxy heard the boy's neck snap. The priest crossed himself and walked down the steps.

"No!" Edward Sughrue screamed, and fell to his knees. Judge Tyler stepped away from him. Sheriff Homer ran over and plucked the gun from Sughrue's limp hand.

Jerry Sughrue's body swung back and forth for a few moments, before coming to a stop.

"Done," Angie said.

She and Roxy went down the stairs. It would be somebody else's job to cut the boy down.

The crowd made room for them as they walked across to where Sughrue was kneeling on the ground sobbing, surrounded by the sheriff and his deputies. Off to the side stood Judge Tyler, who seemed unfazed by the entire situation.

"Nicely done," he said to Angie.

"Weren't you worried he'd kill you?" Sheriff Homer asked the judge.

"No," Tyler said.

"Come on, Mr. Sughrue," Homer said. "You're under arrest."

"What are you arresting him for?" Tyler asked.

"Threatenin' you, tryin' to stop a legal hangin' . . . I'll come up with somethin' else."

"Don't arrest him," Tyler said.

"What?"

"Not for threatening me," Tyler said.

"You can arrest him for having my father killed," Angie suggested.

"Can you prove it?" Tyler asked her.

"Didn't he confess just a few minutes ago?" Angie asked.

Tyler looked at her, then at Homer.

"Maybe he did," Tyler said. "All right, put him in a cell and talk to him about it when he stops bawling."

"Let's go get a drink," Roxy said to Angie. "I can use one."

"So can I," Angie said.

She watched the two deputies lift Sughrue off the ground and take him into the sheriff's office, then followed Roxy away.

Chapter Twenty-Nine

Roxy and Angie repaired to the Hellion Saloon. They got sidelong glances from the other patrons, but nobody looked directly at them or said a word. After all, they had just watched Angie hang a man. Not what anyone expected of a woman.

They each had a shot of whiskey and a beer. Angie tossed down her whiskey, but since Roxy didn't often imbibe, she sipped hers and followed it with beer.

"You okay?" Roxy asked.

"Honestly?" Angie said. "I'm glad I had a light breakfast. When his neck snapped . . ."

"I know." They each drank again. "What now, Angie?" Roxy asked.

"Well," she said, "I haven't mentioned this, but my father had several more jobs scheduled."

"And you plan to see them through?"

"I think I should."

"What's the next stop?" Roxy asked.

"A town called Ludlow, still in Arizona, and then across the border into New Mexico at a place called Rio Rancho."

"I spent some time in Santa Fe," Roxy said, "think I passed Rio Rancho."

"You want to come along?"

"Are you expecting trouble?"

"Not like this, I hope," she said, "but I don't assume a hangman is ever welcome."

Roxy thought, and then shrugged. She still had no clue where to look next for her father, and she liked Angie's company.

"Sure, why not?" she said. "I might as well tag along and keep you alive a little while longer."

"I'll drink to that."

They clinked their beer glasses.

Sheriff Homer came through the batwing doors, spotted them and walked over.

"The body's been taken to the undertaker," he told them.

"I don't particularly care where it was taken to, Sheriff," Angie said. "My job is done."

"Yes, it is," Homer said. "I just thought you'd like to know that Edward Sughrue has admitted he sent some men after your father. He claims they weren't supposed to kill him. Apparently, things got out of hand."

"Did he say who the men were?" Angie asked.

"Yeah, and it looks like you and Miss Doyle already took care of them, in your hotel."

128

"Kirk wasn't involved in that?" Roxy asked.

"No, apparently," Homer said, "Kirk was just sent after you."

"So the same bushwhackers who came after me killed my father."

"That's it."

"Then I guess I really am done here," Angie said.

"Except for this," Homer said, reaching into his pocket. "Your fee."

"Thanks," she said, tucking the bills away. "I guess we're done."

"Is that true?" Homer asked. "Are you gonna be able to leave Sughrue to the law?"

"Are you charging him?" Roxy asked.

"That's gonna be up to the judge," Homer said, "but it looks like it."

"Then we'll be leaving town tomorrow, Sheriff," Angie said. "I just need a good meal and a good night's sleep."

"Can't say I'll be sorry to see you ladies go," Homer admitted.

"Can't say we'll be sorry to put this place behind us," Roxy retorted.

"Looks like there's nothing else to be said," Homer replied, and left.

"What if they decide to let Sughrue go?" Roxy asked Angie.

"We'll be gone. We won't even know if they do that. But if they do, what's left for him? You saw him. He's a broken man."

"And that's enough for you?"

"I told you before," Angie said. "I didn't want to kill him. I wanted him to suffer, and see his son die."

"Seems like a fitting punishment, to me," Roxy added.

"Another beer?" Angie asked. "My treat. I'll even go to the bar and get it."

"Let's do it."

***

Sheriff Homer went from the Hellion Saloon right to Judge Tyler's chambers, where the clerk let him right in.

"Where are they?" Tyler asked.

"The Hellion."

"Doing what?"

"Drinkin'," Homer said. "I guess they're celebratin'."

"They tell you their plans?"

"Said they're leavin' town in the mornin'."

"That's good news," Tyler said.

"What do you wanna do with Mr. Sughrue, Judge?" Homer asked.

"Just hold him in a cell until they leave," Tyler said, "then let him out."

"You ain't gonna charge him?"

"With what?"

"Killin' the hangman, Blackthorne?"

"That didn't happen here."

"Then holdin' a gun on you, this mornin'?"

Judge Tyler pointed a finger at Homer and said, "That didn't happen either, understand?"

"Then what about tryin' to stop the hangin'?" Sheriff Homer asked.

"What else would a father do?" Tyler asked. "You got any other bright ideas?"

"Well, no, but . . ."

"But what?"

"What if Blackthorne finds out you let him go?" Homer asked.

"And how will she find that out?" Tyler asked. "Are you going to tell her?"

"No, 'course not."

"Then get the hell out of here and go to work," Tyler said. "Let me do my job."

"Sure, Judge," Homer said, "Whatever you say."

"You got that right, whatever I say," Judge Tyler told him.

As Homer left, Tyler turned his attention to a list of names on his desk. Once they removed Sughrue as "City Manager," they were going to need a real Mayor.

Chapter Thirty

Roxy and Angie agreed to meet in the hotel lobby for supper. After that, they'd go their own ways, since there was no reason for anyone to want to harm Angie, anymore. The hanging was in the past.

Roxy actually decided to go to her room and get some sleep. Even though the boy had been hanged, she still blocked her door with a wooden chair. Angie may be safe, but there was always somebody who wanted to put a bullet into Lady Gunsmith.

Angie, on the other hand, didn't want to go to her room. Alone. She felt the need to unwind, and only knew of one way to do it.

She stopped in the lobby, where Dennis sat slouching behind the desk. When he saw her, he straightened up rather quickly.

"Can you get away?" she asked.

"Um, when?"

"Now, silly boy," she said. "Right now."

He straightened even more.

"I'll have to get somebody to cover for me."

"I'll wait upstairs," she said, "but don't take too long, or I might get somebody else to cover me."

"I'll be there!" he said, enthusiastically.

Angie went upstairs to wait . . .

***

When the knock came at her door Angie padded naked to it and asked, "Who is it?"

"Um, Dennis? From downstairs? You told me to come up?"

She opened it and stood there naked, staring at him. His eyes widened as he took in all that creamy skin, the large, brown tipped breasts and wide hips, and the tangle of golden hair between her thighs.

"It's about time, young man," she said. "I was about to start without you."

"Um—" he said, but that was as far as he got before she reached out and pulled him inside. She slammed the door and pushed him down on the bed, on his back. The only part of him she had any interest in was in his pants. She didn't think she had even kissed him the first time they were together. Except for his excellent cock, he was still like a little boy.

But that young cock was strong and hard even before she took his boots and trousers off. She got to her knees and gobbled him into her mouth, sucking avidly, wetting his penis and getting it even harder.

"Wait, wait, can I get my shirt—"

"Shh," she said, sliding her hand up under his shirt, then pulling it away. She didn't like his concave chest. "Just lie still and keep quiet."

"Quiet?"

"Yes, quiet," she said. "I don't want the whole hotel to know what we're doing." What she meant was she didn't want Roxy to hear them.

She went back to what she was doing, bending her head and taking his young cock into her mouth. He gasped and bit his lip to obey her and keep quiet.

When she had him good and hard, she slid into his lap, reaching down to hold him steady. She held him tight and slid down on him, taking him inside, then started riding him. Her big breasts bobbed about, so that Dennis' attention was divided between watching them, and trying to match her bouncing movements.

"Ooooh, yeah," she groaned, also trying to keep quiet, "this is what I needed . . . mmmmm, yeah . . . faster, move your hips faster . . . right, right . . ."

Dennis finally couldn't resist and started to reach for her. She allowed him to grope her, squeeze her breasts and tweak her nipples until she felt that big wave of pleasure flooding over her, then slapped his hands away and bounced on him uncontrollably . . .

Chapter Thirty-One

"I've changed my mind," Angie said to Roxy later, over supper.

"About leaving tomorrow?" Roxy asked.

After Angie had finished with Dennis and kicked the poor confused boy out of her room, she had relaxed in her bed and done some thinking. She was now relating to Roxy.

"No," she said, "I still want to leave, but first I want to see Edward Sughrue."

"Why?"

"I want to see him in jail, and talk to him," she said.

"And where do you want me?"

Angie reached across the table and took Roxy's hand.

"You've been a great source of comfort and security to me, Roxy. I'd like you with me, but if you don't want to come, I'll understand."

"I don't have a problem with it," Roxy said. "I just didn't want to intrude."

"You could never be an intrusion," Angie said. "I have to tell you, you're my only friend."

"Then I'll be there."

"Thanks."

"When do you want to do that? Tonight or in the morning?" Roxy asked.

"Let's do it in the morning."

"And what about tonight?"

"I don't particularly want to do anything tonight," Angie said. "I'll just stay in my room. You can go to a saloon, if you want."

"I don't know what the mood of this town is after a hanging," Roxy said. "Could be men will stay away from me, or maybe somebody will want a fight. I'm all for staying inside."

"Poker?" Angie asked.

Roxy shrugged and said, "Why not? That is, unless you're going to have company?"

"No," Angie said, "not me. You?"

"Even if I wanted some," Roxy said, "I wouldn't know who. And I don't particularly want to go to a saloon and just pick somebody out."

"Well," Angie said, "there's always Dennis."

"He's kind of a boy," Roxy said.

"I'm older than you," Angie said, "so sometimes a young tallywacker is tempting. And his is young and, uh, kind of long."

"I think I'm going to leave Dennis to you, Angie," Roxy said. "I think he'd be kind of disappointing after a man like Kirk."

"Too bad you had to kill Kirk, then," Angie said.

"That was his choice, not mine," Roxy pointed out.

"True. So, what should we play for this time?"

Roxy looked around the hotel dining room, then suggested, "Let's get a bunch of toothpicks on the way out."

***

Angie suggested they play poker in Roxy's room. She didn't want Roxy, her friend, to see the messy sheets on her bed. They played until late into the night, then turned in, agreeing to meet in the lobby to check out of their rooms and have breakfast. Angie suggested they retrieve their horses from the livery, and then go to the sheriff's office to see Edward Sughrue. Roxy decided to let her call the play and just go along.

Angie had awakened that morning feeling refreshed, and also something unexpected, as well. She was replaying the moment of hanging Jerry Sughrue over and over in her head, and where the day before it had made her feel slightly sick, she found today that she liked the feeling. It was odd, but she was now looking forward to going to the next town for the next hanging. She decided this was not something she should confide to Roxy. She had never heard her father say that he liked his job, but she wondered now if that was just something he kept to himself?

When they entered the sheriff's office, Homer looked up at them in surprise.

"What brings you ladies here this mornin'?" he asked. "Come to say goodbye?"

"I want to talk to Sughrue," Angie said.

"Why?" he asked.

"Maybe I want to rub his face in what I did," she said. "Or maybe I just want to see him in a cell."

"Well," he said, sitting back, "considering the effect he's had on your life, I don't see why not. Do you want to actually go into the cell?"

"No," she said, "I'll just stand on the outside and look in. I think that makes more sense."

"And Lady Gunsmith?" Homer asked.

"I'm just along for the ride, Sheriff," Roxy said. "Outside the cell is fine."

"Well then, go on ahead," Homer said. "Just leave your guns on my desk."

Angie put her rifle on the desk, but Roxy said, "I'll keep mine, if you don't mind. I'll just stand far enough back from the cell that he can't reach it."

"Suit yourself," Homer said. "It's my guess that you always do."

Chapter Thirty-Two

Angie entered the cell block with Roxy close behind her. Fittingly, Edward Sughrue was occupying the same cell his son had been in. He was sitting on the pallet with his head in his hands. When he heard them, he looked up. His hair was a jagged white mess, his eyes haunted. He looked as if he had aged ten years.

"Have you come to gloat?" he asked her.

"As a matter of fact," Angie said, "that's exactly why I'm here."

"I suppose I deserve that," he said. "Why didn't you just kill me yesterday?"

"Because then you wouldn't be suffering," Angie said.

He stared at her, then said, "You're a hard woman. I guess you need that in your line of work."

"You had my father needlessly killed," she reminded him. "What else do you expect from me?"

"It *was* needless," he agreed. "That's what I get for sending idiots to do a job."

"The same idiots who tried to bushwhack me," Angie said. "The same idiots who tried to kill Roxy Doyle and me in our rooms."

"Yes, yes . . . yes!" Sughrue yelled the last word. "Are you happy? Yes, I did all that to try to save my son."

"I *am* happy," Angie said. "As happy as I can be, having lost my father. Happy that you lost your son, and you're sitting in a cell."

"Then leave me be," Sughrue said, putting his head in his hands again. "Leave me be or kill me."

"Believe me," Angie said to him, "I'm tempted to kill you, Sughrue, but I think I'll do the first one. I'll leave you be in your cell, and your misery."

Sughrue had stopped listening. He had his hands over his ears, now, and was rocking back and forth, making a high, keening sound.

"I think he's lost his mind," Roxy said, speaking for the first time.

"Good," Angie said, "then we're done, here."

She turned and walked past Roxy out of the cell block. Roxy stared at Sughrue for a few more moments, then turned and followed.

As Angie picked up her rifle from the sheriff's desk he asked, "Anythin' else?"

"No," Angie said, "we're done, here."

She turned and walked out, followed by Roxy. They mounted their horses and rode out of Copper City.

***

Once Lady Gunsmith and the hang "lady" left his office, Sheriff Homer gave them enough time to clear the city limits before grabbing the key from the wall and entering the cell block.

"All right, Mr. Sughrue," he said, unlocking the cell door. "Up."

Sughrue looked up at Homer in confusion. Did the sheriff intend to shoot him, saying he was trying to escape? The gallows was still standing, maybe they were planning on hanging him?

"What are you doing?" he asked.

"I'm lettin' you go home," Homer said.

"What?"

"You heard me," Homer said. "Go home, get out . . . leave!"

"But . . . why?"

"The Judge's orders," Homer said, "and I don't question Judge Tyler. If you want, you can go to his chambers and ask him why."

Edward Sughrue struggled to his feet, stared at the now wide open cell door and asked, "But what am I supposed to do now?"

"It's not my job to tell you that," Sheriff Homer said. "I've got my own problems."

Homer walked out of the cell block, not caring whether Sughrue stayed or left.

***

Sughrue continued to stare at the open door, something he hadn't expected he would see for quite some time. If he walked through it, and was free, what then?

Slowly, he shuffled forward and stepped out of the cell. When he entered the office, Sheriff Homer didn't even look at him. He wasn't even sure the lawman's eyes were open.

He increased the tempo of his steps as he approached the front door, and then when he opened it and stepped out, he stopped and took a deep breath. The sun was bright, the air crisp, his son was dead, but he was still alive. There had to be a reason for that.

He needed to figure out why he'd been spared. But before he could do that, he decided he needed a bath and a change of clothes. Once he was feeling human again, maybe he'd start to understand why he was still alive.

Chapter Thirty-Three

Ludlow was a day's ride from Copper City, which meant one night on the trail. They alternated between chattering away for hours to riding in total silence, each alone with their thoughts. When they agreed to camp, they divvied up the chores, Roxy starting the fire and getting a pot of coffee going, Angie seeing to the horses.

By the time Angie was done, the smell of coffee was thick in the air, and Roxy had put a pan of beans on the fire.

"I'm starving," Angie said. "Even those beans look good."

"Almost ready," Roxy said, handing her a cup of coffee.

"Thanks."

They sat across the fire from each other. When the beans were ready, Roxy dished them out equally and handed Angie a plate and fork.

"Thanks."

"How much time have you spent on the trail?" Roxy asked.

"Not as much as you, I'm sure," Angie said. "I only came west a short time ago after being at school in the East, and then I was married."

"That's the first time you've mentioned being married," Roxy pointed out.

"It was a mistake, and it's what kept me from coming back to be with my father after school," Angie explained. "He was a vile brute who beat me one time too often, so I hit him with a frying pan and left."

"Good for you."

"From that point on I worked different jobs, trying to save the money to come west."

"Your father couldn't send you some money?"

"Being a hangman is not a well-paying profession," she said. "He offered but I told him to hold onto his money, that I'd get out here on my own."

"How much time did you get to spend with him before he was killed?" Roxy asked.

"Not much," Angie said. "Just a matter of days. I guess if I had let him send me some money, I could've had more time with him."

"I'm sorry."

"Well, look at you," Angie said. "Haven't seen your father for almost half your life, and now you've been looking for years."

"I guess it's stupid," Roxy said. "I'm old enough now not to need a daddy, but I'd still like to know my father."

"I can't blame you for that," Angie said.

Once they were finished eating, Roxy suggested that Angie get some sleep while she stood watch for a while.

"Are you expecting trouble?" Angie asked.

"I'm always expecting trouble," Roxy said, "which means I'm always careful. I just want to make sure nobody followed us from Copper City."

"Who do you think would've followed us?" Angie asked.

"Like I said," Roxy went on, "I'm just being careful. I don't expect any trouble because of the hanging, but maybe just because of who *I* am."

"Well, you backed me all the way when it seemed they were going to be coming after me," Angie said, "it's only fair that I back you if somebody's after Lady Gunsmith."

"Believe me," Roxy said, "if I hear anything, I'll wake you, but I'm only going to stay up a little while, and then get some sleep myself."

"Well, if you decide you want me to stand watch, just wake me up and I'll do it," Angie said.

"I will," Roxy said. "I promise."

As Angie covered herself up in her bedroll and tried to get comfortable, Roxy put on another pot of coffee and sat down in front of the fire.

Roxy was concerned that, during the parts of the ride that were filled with conversation, it was Angie who did most of the talking. It seemed to Roxy as if hanging the boy was something Angie was dreading, and yet wasn't regretting at all. In fact, she even said at one point she thought her father might've been proud of the way she handled her first job.

Roxy had already agreed to stay with Angie through the next two jobs, but she thought she was probably better off going her own way after that. If Angie was going to start looking forward to hangings, then either she wasn't the person Roxy thought she was, or she was simply changing drastically. Either way, she would no longer be someone Roxy wanted to ride with. Being a hangman, a hang "woman" or simply an executioner was certainly a necessary evil, but it was not a profession to be enjoyed.

But Roxy had never known anyone in that line of work before. Maybe they *did* like their job, but enjoying a job and being good at it were certainly two different things. Roxy was good with a gun, but she sure as hell didn't enjoy using one. If she ever did, she'd have to give serious thought to taking her gun off. Clint Adams himself had told her killing was nothing to enjoy or be proud of. Being good at it simply kept you alive.

Chapter Thirty-Four

Ludlow turned out to be a smaller town than Copper City. Once again, the two women attracted attention riding in for any number of reasons. Two of the most obvious might've been Roxy's red hair, or Angie's noose hanging from her saddle.

Angie decided their first stop should be the local sheriff's office, since they were passing it.

"Might as well let him know we're here," she said.

Roxy nodded and followed. They dismounted in front and tied off their horses. As they entered, a tall, mustachioed, rugged looking man in his late forties was coming out of the cell blocks, carrying a broom. They noticed that his gunbelt was hanging on a wall peg, with the cell keys.

"You ladies caught me cleanin'," he said. "Not a very manly thing to be doin', I know, but I have to do a little of everythin' in this job." He put the broom in a corner and turned to face them. "I'm Sheriff Bill O'Neal. What can I do for you?"

"Sheriff, I'm Angie Blackthorne."

He stared at her, waiting for more.

"I'm here for the hanging?" she said.

"To watch it?" he asked.

"To do it," she said. "I'm the hangman."

"Is that for real?" he asked. "Or are you joshin' me?"

"It's for real," she said. "My father was supposed to do it, but he was killed. I'm taking his place."

"Well, whataya know," he said, shaking his head. "I never expected the hangman to be a pretty woman. Sorry, I don't mean to offend you."

"No offense taken," Angie said.

"And this other lady? Your bodyguard?"

"We're just riding together," Angie said. "This is Roxy Doyle."

"Of course," the sheriff said. "I shoulda known from that red hair. Well, it's gonna be interestin' havin' both of you in town."

"I understand the hanging is scheduled for two days from now," Angie said.

"That's right."

"That'll give me time to check the gallows and get my measurements from the prisoner."

"Well, he's back there waitin' for you," the sheriff said. "He's sleepin' now, like he don't have a care in the world."

"Good for him," Angie said. "We'll go over and check into the hotel now. I assume there's a room waiting for me?"

"Yes, Ma'am," he said, "over at the Horse & Buggy Hotel." He looked at Roxy. "I'm sorry, I guess you'll have to pay for your room, unless you share."

"That's okay," Roxy said. "I can handle it."

"You'll find a livery at the end of the street," the lawman said. "Just tell Gus I sent you over and he'll take care of your horse for free." He looked at Roxy, but she spoke first.

"I know, not mine," she said. "I can pay my own way." Just barely, she added to herself.

The sheriff looked at Angie again.

"You can come in any time you want to get your measurements," he said.

"And where's the gallows?"

"You'll see 'em, just outside the livery," he told her.

"Fine."

"Also," he said, as they headed for the door, "you can get your meals in the hotel dining room, or the Big Horn Café down the street. Again, just tell 'em who you are."

"I will," Angie said.

"And I tell you what," he said, again before they could leave. "If you'll meet me at the Big Horn later today, it'd be my pleasure to buy you both supper."

Angie and Roxy exchanged a glance, and then Angie said, "That's right nice of you, Sheriff. Six o'clock?"

"Six, is fine, ladies," he said. "I'll see you then."

This time they managed to get out the door before he could speak again.

"I think he likes you," Roxy said, as they mounted up to ride to the livery.

"That's funny," Angie said, "I was going to say the same thing to you."

They laughed as they rode down the street . . .

***

The livery and hotel were no trouble at all. Once Angie mentioned "Gus," the hostler was happy to take both their horses. At the hotel the desk clerk had them both register in the book, then handed them their keys.

"Of course, Miss Blackthorne, your room will be paid for by the town."

"Thank you."

As they walked up the stairs with their saddlebags and rifles Angie said to Roxy, "You know, we could've shared my free room."

"I like my privacy," Roxy said, "but I'll be happy to enjoy a free meal later."

"So will I," Angie said, "especially with that rugged looking sheriff."

Chapter Thirty-Five

The sheriff was already at the café with a table waiting for them. He had his hat off and had obviously combed his hair and his bushy mustache. He stood as they approached.

"Ladies," he said, "thanks for joinin' me."

Both Angie and Roxy had washed up and put on fresh shirts after their ride on the trail. And they had both run a brush through their hair, so that when they removed their hats, their hair fell to their shoulders in waves.

"You both look lovely," he said, "even after a hard ride on the trail."

"Thank you," Angie said.

The man was rough-hewn, but also had a rustic charm to him that they both found appealing.

They all sat, and a waiter came scurrying over.

"Sheriff? Ladies, welcome."

"Would you ladies mind if I ordered for all of us?" the sheriff asked.

"Not at all," Angie said. "You know the menu."

"We'll have the pork chops, Harry," the sheriff said to the waiter. "With vegetables and biscuits. Ladies, coffee or beer?"

"Beer," they both said.

"You heard the ladies," Sheriff O'Neal said.

"Yes, sir."

"I'm a little surprised, Miss Blackthorne, that you haven't asked me anything about the prisoner."

"All I need to know about him I'll learn when I measure him, Sheriff."

"You don't want to know his name, or what he was convicted of?"

"It's not important to what I do," Angie said.

"And you, Miss Doyle? Do you feel the same way?"

"I'm not curious, if that's what you mean," she said. "Whatever his name is, I assume he was convicted of murder in order to be hanged."

"Well, it seems I'm never too old to learn somethin' new," he said. "Two women who aren't curious."

"Women aren't all the same, Sheriff," Angie said.

"And I'm findin' that out," he admitted.

The more the man talked the more Roxy and Angie were discovering they didn't like him. He even commented on the fact that they didn't talk much "like most women."

"Sheriff," Angie said, when they finished eating, "we appreciate the meal, but we did ride all day and we're kind of tired."

"Of course," he said, "you need your rest. I'll pay the bill and walk you out."

Out on the boardwalk in front of the café they thanked him again for supper and told him they would see him in the morning. He kept his hat in his hand until they started to walk off.

***

As they reached the hotel, they stopped for a moment outside before going in.

"I don't like him," Angie said.

"The sheriff?" Roxy said. "I don't, either."

"I mean," she said, "I wouldn't throw him out of my bed, but he would have to shut up."

"And what are the chances of that?" Roxy asked. "Seems to me he always talks."

"And says the wrong thing."

"Right."

"So, I want you to know I'm not going to try to get him into my bed."

"Uh-huh."

"I mean, in case you were thinking—"

"I wasn't," Roxy said.

"Well . . . good."

They entered the hotel and went up to their rooms.

***

Later, Roxy came back down, intending to go to a saloon and have a beer, maybe unwind a bit. It was just too early to stay in her room until morning.

A couple of blocks from the hotel she found the Rusty Lantern Saloon and went in. It was small, no girls, no games, just whiskey and beer. The few patrons in the place watched as she walked to the bar.

"Beer," she said.

"Comin' up," the bartender said.

He set a cold beer in front of her and then remained there, looking at her.

"Can I do something for you?" she asked.

"Haven't seen you around here before," the heavyset man said. "Just ride in?"

"That's right."

"Then you're just in time."

"For what?"

"We got us a hanging scheduled."

"Is that a fact?"

"It is," he said. "You ever seen a hangin' before?"

"As a matter of fact," she lied, "I haven't."

"Well, you're in for a treat," he said. "The whole town's gonna turn out for this one."

"Why's that?"

"He killed a child."

"Then I guess he deserves what he gets," she said.

"Oh, he deserves it, all right," the bartender said.

She drank half her beer, looked around the place. Several men were still watching her.

"Don't mind them," the bartender said. "They ain't never seen a woman as pretty as you."

"No pretty women come in here?" Roxy asked.

"I didn't mean in here," he said. "I just mean they ain't never seen anybody as pretty as you . . . ever! Neither have I."

"Well," she said, "thanks for the compliment." She finished her beer, put her hand in her pocket for money.

"That's okay, pretty lady," the barman said. "It's on the house. My name's Max. Come on back in here next time you're thirsty."

"Thank you, Max."

"Maybe see you at the hangin'?" he called, "day after tomorrow."

"Yeah," she called back, "maybe."

Chapter Thirty-Six

"A child killer?" Angie asked.

"That's what the bartender said," Roxy replied.

They were having breakfast the next morning in the hotel. Roxy told Angie about going out for a beer.

"I was just restless," Roxy went on, "ordered a beer from a talkative bartender. He told me."

"Then I guess he deserves to be hanged," Angie said. "After breakfast we'll go get his measurements, and then look at the gallows."

"Right."

The waitress brought their bacon-and-eggs and they set about eating.

***

When they entered the sheriff's office, he was seated behind his desk. He smiled when he saw them.

"Ladies," he said, "are you here for your measurements?"

"That's right, Sheriff," Angie said.

"Have you looked at the gallows yet?"

"Not yet," Angie said. "That'll be our next stop."

"Let's get this done, then," he said, standing and grabbing the cell key from the wall. "Leave your guns on my desk."

"I'll stand back," Roxy said.

O'Neal turned and looked at her, then said, "Oh, right."

He went into the cell block with Angie behind him. Roxy stood at the doorway to watch.

The man in the cell was very different from the last prisoner she had watched Angie measure. Jerry Sughrue was a skinny young kid. This man—this child killer— was a large strapping man in his thirties.

"Henry," the sheriff said, "you're gonna stand still and let this lady do her job. If you don't, I will lay you out on the floor and let her do it that way. Understood?"

"Job? What job?" he demanded.

"She has to measure you for the gallows."

"Why her?" the man asked. "Why not the hangman?"

"Because," the sheriff said, "she *is* the hangman."

The man stared at Angie.

"What?" he asked. "A woman is gonna hang me?"

"That's right. Now stand back and hold still."

Henry took two steps back and then stopped. Sheriff O'Neal unlocked the cell door.

"If you try anythin'," O'Neal told him, "she won't have to hang you, because I'll kill you. Understand?"

"I understand."

The lawman stepped back.

"Go ahead," he told Angie.

She stepped into the cell and, dwarfed by the man, went about taking her measurements. When she was done, she stepped back outside the cell.

"Don't you have to know how much I weigh?" Henry asked her.

"I can guess," she told him. To the sheriff she said, "I'm done."

O'Neal slammed the cell door and locked it.

"And what's her job?" Henry asked, indicating Roxy.

"Never mind," O'Neal told him.

Roxy moved away from the doorway as Angie and the sheriff left the cell block.

"Thanks, Sheriff," Angie said.

"Thomas Henry," the sheriff said.

"What?" Angie asked.

"His name is Thomas Henry," the sheriff said. "I just thought you should know."

"And does he have any relatives who are going to try to stop this hanging?"

"Not a one."

"That's good. We'll be by in the morning to walk him to the gallows."

"Fine."

She and Roxy left the office.

Chapter Thirty-Seven

They had seen the gallows earlier, when taking their horses to the livery the day before. Now they could see that the sheriff had supplied some sandbags for Angie to use in examining the structure.

As they had done in Copper City, Roxy helped her carry the bags up the stairs, then stood aside as Angie tied them to her rope and dropped each bag, of differing weights, through the trap door.

"It's solid," Angie said.

"That's good, because he's a big man," Roxy said.

"Weighs at least two hundred and fifty pounds," Angie judged.

"Luckily, we don't have to carry him."

Angie glanced down and saw some people looking up at them, curiously.

"Nothing to see here!" she shouted. "Come back tomorrow."

They moved on.

"I don't understand the fascination with hangings," Roxy said.

"They're a crowd pleaser, that's for sure," Angie said. "My father told me stories about hangings that brought out drummers, performers, pick pockets, every low life you could possibly think of to work the crowds."

They descended the gallows, moved the sandbags over to one side. Roxy noticed that Angie had left her rope and noose hanging there, ready to be used.

"What now?" Roxy asked.

"Now," Angie said, "lunch."

***

They found a small café and had a simple lunch of sandwiches.

"I'm worried about you," Roxy said, as they finished.

"Oh? Why's that?"

"You don't seem upset anymore about hanging Jerry Sughrue. I've been watching and listening to you since then. Angie, I think you're looking forward to this one."

Angie stared at Roxy for a few moments, then leaned forward.

"When that kid's neck snapped, I felt sick. But pretty quickly, it changed. I don't know why. I hadn't decided, you know, whether I was going to keep doing my father's job. But now . . . I kind of like the idea."

"Of hanging people?"

"People who deserve it," she said. "People who've been tried and sentenced." She shrugged. "What's wrong with that?"

"There's nothing wrong with doing a job," Roxy said. "But enjoying it—"

"Look, Roxy," Angie said, "why don't we do the job tomorrow, and then we can talk about whether or not I'm going to continue. If I do, I don't expect you to stay with me. At some point you're going to start looking for your father again?"

"That's right."

"I understand that," Angie said. "Believe me, I do. I know if this job becomes something I actually enjoy, it's going to change the way you think about me. Hell, it'll change the way I think about me." She sat back in her chair. "After this one I'll just need some time."

"That's okay, Angie," Roxy said. "I'm not judging you—I'm trying not to judge you."

"How about a beer?" Angie asked. "There's no reason we can't go to one of the saloons in town. Apparently, this prisoner doesn't have any family who's going to try to kill me to save him."

"Beer sounds good," Roxy said.

***

Roxy took Angie to the Rusty Lantern Saloon, where Max the bartender was still behind the bar.

"Hey, the pretty lady is back," he said, as they approached the bar, "and she brought another pretty lady. What can I get you?"

"We'll take beer, Max," Roxy said. "Thanks."

Max set two beers down on the bar. It was still early afternoon, and the place was mostly empty. The men who were there were looking at Roxy and Angie.

"Didn't think I'd see you til the hanging," Max said to Roxy.

"You're going to the hanging?" Angie asked.

"The whole town will be there," Max said. "What about you? Will you be there?"

"Me?" Angie said. "Oh, I'll be there." She sipped her beer. "See, I'm doing the hanging."

Max looked shocked. Angie looked at Roxy and grinned. Roxy thought whether Angie enjoyed the actual job or not, she certainly enjoyed the reactions.

Chapter Thirty-Eight

"I tell you what," Angie said, when they got back to their hotel. "Let's do supper on our own later and meet in the lobby in the morning for the hanging. That'll give me time to myself to think."

"Fine with me," Roxy said. "I could use some time to myself, too. In fact, I might go and talk to the sheriff, see if he's heard anything about my father."

"That's good," Angie said. "Maybe you can get a lead. I hope he can help."

"I'm going to start with him, and then talk to some bartenders."

"I hope it pans out," Angie said.

"Think real hard about what you're going to do, Angie," Roxy advised.

"Oh, I will," Angie said. "I'm going to give it a helluva lot of thought."

"See you tomorrow," Roxy said.

Angie went into the hotel, and Roxy headed for the sheriff's office.

***

"Back so soon?" Sheriff O'Neal asked. "Where's your friend?"

"We have our own lives," Roxy said, "our own business."

"So you're here on your own business, this time?" O'Neal asked.

"That's right."

"Well, have a seat and tell me how I can help."

She sat across from him.

"I'm looking for my father," she said. "I was wondering if you'd heard anything about him being in this area?"

"Your father?" O'Neal said. "Who would that be, and why would I have heard about him?"

"He's Gavin Doyle."

The lawman raised his eyebrows.

"The bounty hunter?"

"That's him."

"I don't know why that surprises me," he said. "The Lady Gunsmith's father is the infamous bounty hunter, Gavin Doyle." He shook his head. "To tell you the truth I thought he was dead. Wouldn't he be kind of old now?"

"Sixty or so," Roxy said.

"And he's still active?"

"From what I hear," she said.

"When's the last time you saw him?"

"I was a little girl," she said. "When I was fifteen, I went out on my own to try and find him. I'm still trying."

"Gavin Doyle," he said. "If he was in the area, I'd probably hear about it."

"That's what I was thinking."

"But I haven't. Like I said, I would've thought he was dead by now."

"Then I won't bother you anymore," Roxy said.

"Hey sheriff!" Thomas Henry called from his cell. "I wanna talk to that redhaired gal."

"Shut up, Henry!" O'Neal called back.

"I got somethin' to tell her!" Henry shouted. "Ask her if she wants to know."

O'Neil looked at Roxy.

"I might as well listen to what he has to say," she said. "I'm here."

"I'll need your gun."

She stared at him.

"I know, you'll stand back," he said. "Go ahead."

She stood up and walked to the cell block. Thomas Henry was standing up against the bars. She stood back, out of his reach.

"What's on your mind, Mr. Henry?"

"You're Gavin Doyle's kid?"

"That's right."

"Sonofabitch."

"Do you know my father?"

"I do," Henry said. "And I can tell you how to find him."

"How?" she asked. "Where is he?"

"Well," Henry said, a crafty look coming over his face, "before I tell you that, you have to do somethin' for me."

"Like what?"

"Like get me outta here," he said. "Keep me from gettin' hung."

"I can't do that."

"Then I can't help ya."

"Which puts me right back where I was before I came in here," she said. "Thanks, anyway."

She went back out to the sheriff.

"He's lyin', you know," O'Neal said. "He just wants you to break him out."

"I'm going to ask around, Sheriff," she said. "If he's not lying, then somebody else will have heard something."

"I hope you're right," Sheriff O'Neal said. "I hope you find out something. I don't want you comin' back here to try and get him out."

Chapter Thirty-Nine

"I'm startin' to think you like me," Max said, as Roxy approached the bar.

"Well, I don't not like you, Max," she said.

"Beer?"

"Sure."

He set her up. The bar was a little busier than the other times she'd been there, but Max remained where he was.

"What's on your mind?" he asked.

"My father."

"Who's your father?" Max asked.

"His name is Gavin Doyle."

"Gavin Do—oh, wait, I knew that already," Max said. "Right, right, Roxy Doyle, Gavin Doyle." He leaned on the bar. "Why are you askin' me about him?"

"Because I'm looking for him," she said. "I've been following rumors about where he is, or sightings. Only now I don't have any. I was wondering if you might've heard his name from somebody in here?"

"Lately? No, I haven't."

"Do you think you could keep your ear to the ground and let me know?"

"Sure, I can do that," Max said.

Roxy drank half her beer.

"Thanks, Max."

"Where's your friend?" Max asked.

"I don't know," Roxy said. "Maybe her room at the hotel."

"I kinda like her."

"Is that right?"

"I mean," Max said, "I like you, too, but you're kinda young for me. Now Miss Blackthorne, she's just the right age for me, don't ya think?"

"What's your point?"

"I'd like to spend some time with her," Max said. "You think you could arrange that?"

Roxy turned to face him, again.

"In return for what?" she asked.

Max shrugged.

"Whatever I can find out."

Roxy came back to the bar and leaned on it.

"How well do you know Thomas Henry?" she asked.

"The man who's gonna hang tomorrow?" Max asked. "He used to come in here from time to time. I know him to say hello and serve him drinks."

"Do you know if he's ever talked about my father?" she asked.

"Hmm," Max said, "Henry and Gavin Doyle? That's interesting."

"So, do you know?"

"No," Max said, "I never heard Henry talk about your father. Why?"

"He's claiming if I stop the hanging, he'll tell me where my father is."

"He's lyin', don't you think?"

"Maybe," Roxy said. "I'll be back, Max."

"Sure," Max said, "and bring your friend."

Roxy turned and left the saloon.

***

Roxy knocked on Angie's door, then knew she was waking her up when she had to knock again. Either that or she wasn't alone. When the door opened Angie squinted at her.

"Guess I was asleep," Angie said. "Are you all right. What do you need?"

"Just wanted to ask you," Roxy said, "how you feel about Max, the bartender?"

***

After Roxy left the saloon Max called a man over.

"Yeah?"

"Caleb, who knows everything that happens in this town?" Max asked.

"You do, Max," the tall, skinny man said.

"Who else?"

"Al Corey."

"Will you go find Corey and bring him here?" Max asked. "Tell him, there's a couple of beers in it for him."

"How about me?" Caleb asked.

"Yeah, there's a beer in it for you, too."

"I'll get him here," Caleb promised.

***

"He wants to sleep with me?" Angie asked, sitting on the edge of her bed.

"He didn't say anything about sleep."

Angie was wearing a shirt unbuttoned, and her underwear. Roxy could see her big, solid breasts and thighs, and knew why she would appeal to a man like Max.

"So you want me to sleep with him so you can get some information about your father?"

"No," Roxy said. "I think Henry's lying to me, and I think Max is trying to take advantage."

"Well, well," Angie said, "men who want what they want and don't care how they get it. What else is new?"

Roxy leaned against the wall.

"I'm sorry I woke you," she said. "I'll get out of your hair. There are still some people I can talk to about my father. I just thought—I don't know what I thought."

"Do you want me to come and help?"

"No," Roxy sad, "you should stay here and get your rest. You've got a big day tomorrow."

Roxy opened the door to leave.

"Hey."

"Yeah?"

"Max," she said, "he's that big, brutish looking bar-tender, right?"

"That's right."

"Why isn't he interested in you?" Angie asked.

Roxy grinned.

"He says I'm too young for him."

"Wow," Angie said, "how flattering."

Chapter Forty

Roxy went to some other saloons in town, drank half a beer in each and asked the bartenders if they'd heard anything about Gavin Doyle. More than half of them said, "I thought he was dead."

When she finished with saloons and came up empty, she decided to get something to eat.

***

Angie walked into the Rusty Lantern Saloon. Max saw her right away and smiled.

"You here for a beer?" he asked. "Or somethin' else?"

"I'll start with a beer."

"Comin' up."

He set a cold beer in front of her.

"Roxy told me she was here earlier," Angie said.

"Yeah."

"She told me what you two talked about."

"Her father?"

"No, other things."

"Oh."

"You still interested?"

"Well . . . yeah." His eyes widened. He was a big, hulking man, not handsome, but not ugly. And he'd probably give her a better ride than that young desk clerk, Dennis, had. "Is that somethin' you'd, uh, think about—"

"Let's talk about that later, Max," Angie said. "Right now, I want to talk about Roxy's father."

"Gavin Doyle?"

"That's right. Do you have any information on where he might be?"

"I don't," he said, "but I do have somebody comin' here who might."

"When will he be here?"

"In a little while," Max said. "I have someone out lookin' for him now."

"Then I'll wait," Angie said. "Depending on what he has, maybe we can talk about . . . that other thing."

"Sounds good to me," Max said.

She drained her beer and said, "Then how about another one?"

"Comin' up."

***

Roxy went back to her hotel, but rather than go in, she found a wooden chair outside and sat.

Her original plan had been to help Angie with this hanging, and then go with her to New Mexico for the next. Now she was thinking this would be it. After Angie hanged Thomas Henry, they'd go their own ways. Hopefully, by then, she'd have some idea where to look next for her father.

***

"There he is," Max said to Angie.

She turned and looked as two men came through the batwing doors.

"Here he is, Max," a skinny man said. The other man was shorter, and squat.

"What's this about, Max?" Al Corey asked.

"Al, this here's Angie Blackthorne," Max said. "She's a friend of Roxy Doyle."

"So? Caleb said somethin' about a beer?" Corey said.

"Here ya go." Max put a beer up for Corey and Caleb. "Caleb, take yours to a table."

"Right."

Corey drank half his beer, wiped his mouth, then asked, "What's this about?"

"Gavin Doyle," Angie said. "Tell me what you know about him."

Chapter Forty-One

Roxy didn't know where Angie was when she turned in for the night. But, as they had arranged, they met in the lobby the next morning for breakfast.

She remembered the light breakfast Angie had eaten before hanging Jerry Sughrue. However, this morning she had a full steak-and-egg breakfast and consumed it with vigor.

"I talked to Max last night," Angie told Roxy.

"Talked?"

"Sure," Angie said. "Oh, I might sleep with the guy before we leave town, but I wouldn't have sex with him for information. That'd make me a whore."

"Angie—"

"Forget it, Roxy," Angie said. "You didn't ask me to sleep with him, you just told me what he said. Anyway, I went to see him."

"Did he find out anything?"

"He brought in another man named Al Corey, who claims to know everything that's going on in the area."

"And?"

"According to him, Gavin Doyle was seen north of here, in a town called Griggsville."

"What was he doing?"

"Outfitting himself at the mercantile there," Angie said. "Corey said it looked like he was on the hunt."

"Griggsville," Roxy said. "I never heard of it."

"According to Corey, there's a mercantile and not much else, so lots of riders stop there for supplies."

"Well," Roxy said, "it looks like I'll be heading north from here, and not going with you to New Mexico."

"That's fine," Angie said. "I knew we'd be parting ways at some point. Let's just finish our breakfast and get this Thomas Henry's neck stretched. That is, unless you think he knows something you need?"

"I think he was lying, trying to get me to save him," Roxy said. "I don't have a problem with you doing your job."

They finished eating and headed over to the jail.

***

There were people crowded in front of the sheriff's office, some holding signs that said "Child Killer." Roxy was certain there would be even more of a crowd at the gallows.

When the mob saw the two women approaching, however, they parted to let them pass. As Roxy and Angie entered, Sheriff O'Neal gave them a big smile.

180

"Big mornin'," he said. "We haven't hanged a child killer—well, ever."

"Just out of curiosity," Roxy said, "what child did he kill?"

"Well," the sheriff said, "as far as I'm concerned, he didn't kill a child. It was a fifteen-year-old who thought he was Billy the Kid. Henry showed him he wasn't. But the town didn't like it, and neither did the judge. He threw the book at 'im."

"Let's get him out of there," Angie said. "You got chains?"

"I do," O'Neil said. "Would you like me to do the honors?"

"Why not?"

O'Neal went into the cell block, put the chains on Thomas Henry's wrists and walked him out. The man looked at Roxy hopefully.

"You think about what I said?" he asked.

"Yes," she said.

"And?"

"You're lying."

"Now wait—"

"I don't appreciate it," Roxy said. "You heard me talking to the sheriff about my father and you jumped at the chance. You're a killer and a liar."

"Look, I know—"

"Forget it, Henry," Angie said, grabbing his arm. "Time to go."

They walked Thomas Henry to the front door and outside. Angie stood to his right, Roxy to his left and the sheriff took up the rear.

People began to shout at him, calling him names and cursing him, as the women walked him down the street toward the gallows. As they reached it, the people parted and let them through, while continuing to call the prisoner names.

"It's all right, Sheriff," Angie said, "we've got it from here."

Angie and Roxy walked the man up the steps, where Roxy stopped. Angie took him to the trap door, slipped the noose around his neck. Once again, there was a priest there reading scripture, but Angie ignored him. Roxy looked down at the crowd and saw a man in a black suit standing in front of everybody. She was willing to bet this was the judge.

There was nothing for Angie to say, except to ask Henry if he wanted a hood.

"Yes," he said, "not because I'm scared, but because I don't want these sons-of-bitches to see my face while I'm hangin' here."

"Whatever the reason is, I don't care," Angie said. She slid a black hood over his head, then stepped back to the lever, and threw it.

The trap door dropped open . . .

Chapter Forty-Two

As Thomas Henry's body swung from side-to-side, the crowd began to thin. Finally, the only person standing there was the judge and one more man.

"Okay, Doc," the judge said, "check him."

The doctor ducked beneath the gallows so he could check the now stationary body.

"He's dead," he said, turning to the judge.

"Then he's the undertaker's, now," the judge said. "Better get him over here, Sheriff."

"Yessir."

The judge turned and walked away.

Angie and Roxy came down from the gallows.

"I'm done," Angie said. "I need to get paid."

"I know," the sheriff said, "and you two are going to move on, right?"

"That's right, Sheriff."

"Well, it was . . . interestin' meetin' you both."

"Yeah, same here," Angie said.

"Come with me to my office and I'll pay you."

***

Roxy and Angie left Ludlow together, but outside of town they split.

"So you're heading for Griggsville?" Angie asked.

"Yeah," Roxy said. "It's probably like most rumors, but I've got to check it out."

"I don't blame you."

"And you'll be in Rio Rancho?" Roxy asked.

"Yep, I've got a job to do there."

"And after that?"

"I don't know," Angie said. "I'll have to take the time to figure it out."

The two women remained on horseback, shook hands, and then went their separate ways. Roxy thought they hadn't dismounted and embraced because they assumed they'd see each other once again.

***

Griggsville was, indeed, nothing but a mercantile that not only sold supplies, but also had a small bar in the back. Other than that, there were some worn out, dilapidated buildings. The place looked more like a ghost town than anything else.

Roxy tied her horse off out front. Above the door it said DELANEY BROTHERS MERCANTILE. She went inside. There was a man behind the counter, and a man behind the bar. They looked enough alike for her to figure they were the brothers. Both were in their fifties.

"Can we help ya, little lady?" the man behind the counter asked. He looked like the older brother.

"Yes," Roxy said, "you *can not* call me 'little lady' again."

"Sorry about that," the man said. "Didn't mean no offense. What can we do for you . . . Miss?"

"I'm looking for a man and heard he might've been here sometime in the past few weeks."

"What's his name?"

"Gavin Doyle."

From the bar the other brother said, "Gavin Doyle, the bounty hunter?"

She turned to him and said, "That's right."

"Who wants to know?" he asked.

"Roxy Doyle," she said. "I'm his daughter."

"Oh," the older brother said, "you're the one they call Lady Gunsmith. I didn't know you were his daughter."

"Well, I am," she said, "and I heard a rumor that he was up this way."

"Barry," the older brother called to the younger, "whataya say?"

"Gavin Doyle, here?" Barry rubbed his jaw. "If he was, he didn't have a drink."

"And he didn't buy any supplies," the other brother said. "Sorry, Miss. I don't think so."

"It's okay," she said. "That's what happens with most rumors."

"Think you could use a cold beer while you're here?" Barry asked.

"As a matter of fact, I do," Roxy said. She walked over to the makeshift bar, which looked to have been constructed from an old wooden door.

"Here ya go," Barry said, setting it down. "On the house."

"Thanks," Roxy said.

Roxy drank the beer, thanked the two men and went outside. As she was mounting up, the older one came running out.

"Hold on, there!" he yelled. "I plumb forgot." He was waving something. "We got a telegraph key here, and you got a telegram. Came in a day or two ago."

"Thank you," she said, taking it from him.

"You can come back inside if you wanna send a reply," he told her.

"I will."

But she didn't want to send a reply. She wanted to ride back to Ludlow.

Chapter Forty-Three

She pushed and cut a day off the trip. She and the horse were both fatigued as she reined in right in front of the sheriff's office.

"That was fast!" O'Neal said, as she entered.

"What happened?"

"It looked like Miss Blackthorne got ambushed outside of town. Must've been soon after you and her went your separate ways."

"Where is she?"

"The hotel," O'Neal said. "The doc's been keepin' an eye on her, but he don't give her much of a chance."

"I'll go and see her."

"I think that's what she's been hangin' on for," Sheriff O'Neal said.

Roxy turned and ran out.

***

The hotel door was unlocked, so she went right in. The desk clerk told her that the doctor was there, with Angie. As she entered, the man turned to look at her. He was tall, silver-haired, dour looking.

"Are you Miss Doyle?" he asked.

"I am."

"She's been waitin' for you," he said. "After bein' shot three times I don't know how, but she has."

Roxy went to the bed and the doctor backed away. Angie was lying on her back, eyes closed, looking very pale.

"Angie?" Roxy said.

Angie opened her eyes and immediately focused on Roxy.

"You came," Angie said.

"As soon as I heard."

"I—I had the sheriff send that telegram to Griggsville," Angie said. "I—I was hoping you'd get here . . . in time."

"I'm here," Roxy said, taking her hand.

"It was him, Roxy."

"Who?"

Angie licked her lips.

"A-after they ambushed me and gunned me down, t-they told me . . . it was him. He sent them."

"Who, Angie?" Roxy asked. "Who sent them?"

"Sughrue," Angie said.

"But he's supposed to be in jail," Roxy said.

Angie closed her eyes and her hand went limp.

"Angie?"

189

Roxy looked at the doctor. He came forward, checked Angie, then shook his head at Roxy.

"You did get here just in time," he told her. "I'm sorry."

Roxy nodded, sat on the edge of the bed.

***

It only took a day to get Angie buried. She had enough money on her to pay for the burial. There was even some left over.

"It's yours," Sheriff O'Neal told her, handing it to Roxy. "She had no family, so . . ."

He also gave her Angie's rifle and horse.

"I'll take the noose, too," Roxy told him.

He picked it up off his desk and handed it to her.

"What are you going to do with that?"

"I'm going to use it for what it was made for," she told him.

"I'm sorry you had to come back here for this," he told her.

"So am I," she said.

"What now?" he asked.

"Now I move on," Roxy said.

"You got a destination in mind?" O'Neal asked.

"Oh yes," Roxy said, "I sure do."

***

She didn't push it. There was no reason to. She was pretty sure Sughrue would still be in Copper City when she got there.

She camped just outside of town, sat at the fire holding the noose in her hand. Other than Clint Adams, she'd have to say Angie Blackthorne was her only friend. What do you do when somebody kills your only friend?

She set the noose down across her lap, picked up her coffee and sipped it, staring out into the darkness. The answer to the question was, if you knew who killed your only friend, you made them pay.

Somehow, Sughrue had gotten out of jail, recruited a gang of men and sent them after Angie. They might have even waited for Roxy and Angie to split up before they hit.

She wasn't concerned with the men who actually did the shooting. They had no doubt been paid. No, the one who had to pay the price was the man who paid them. And he had done it to avenge his son's death. Roxy avenging Angie's death would bring it full circle.

Chapter Forty-Four

The next morning Roxy left her horse tied to a tree and walked into Copper City. She didn't want to attract any attention.

She thought about waiting until dark, but that would be the waste of a day. She needed to find out what happened with Sughrue, and where he was. She only knew one person who could tell her that.

Tucking her red hair up under her hat, she walked the side streets of Copper City, keeping close to the buildings, trying not to be noticed, and staying away from Main Street. Eventually, she worked her way around to the back of the jail, where the gallows had been erected. It had been almost a month since the hanging. The structure was gone, but she could see marks in the ground where it had stood.

She went to the back door of the jail, tried it, found it unlocked. As she entered, she saw that the cells were empty. She walked past the cells and peered out the door, into the office. Nothing had changed since she left. As usual, Sheriff Homer was sitting at his desk, head lolling to one side as he dozed.

She stepped through the doorway, eased over to him, drew her gun and pressed the barrel to his head. His eyes popped open, immediately.

"Just sit easy." She looked around, saw his gunbelt was hanging on a wall hook.

"Wha—who—" he stammered.

"I'm going to take my gun away from your head," she said. "Just continue to sit still. Understand?"

"Y-yeah."

She eased the gun away, then moved around so she was standing across the desk from him. His eyes widened when he saw her.

"You! You're back?"

"I'm back," she said. "Do you know why?"

"Uh, n-no . . ."

"Guess."

"Um . . . I can't."

"What happened to Sughrue after we left?" she demanded.

"Oh, yeah, that."

"Well?"

He stared at the gun, his eyes a bit glassy.

"The judge told me to let him go," he said.

"So it was the judge's idea?"

"Yes."

"What happened after that?"

"Uh, the judge got Sughrue to step down as the City Manager."

"And then what?"

"Then we elected a mayor."

"You did that in less than a month?"

"Uh, yeah, I guess."

"And what happened to Sughrue?"

"He, uh, went home."

"And stayed there?"

"I guess."

"Is he there now? In his house?"

"I—I suppose so."

"Did you know he sent men after Angie Black-thorne?" she asked.

"B-Blackthorne?"

"The woman who hung his son?"

"Oh, her," Homer said. "N-no, I didn't know anythin' about that."

"You didn't, huh?"

"N—no," he said. "He-he don't confide in me."

"Well, he did," she said. "He sent men to bushwhack her—again!—and this time they killed her."

"Oh . . ."

"So I'll ask you again, Sheriff Homer," she said. "Where is he?"

"He's gotta be at his house," Homer said. "Are you gonna kill 'im?"

"That's the plan."

"Now, you do that, and the judge'll make me come after you," Homer complained.

"Come on, Sheriff," she said, "you're not going to come after me. You'll give up your badge first."

"If that happens, the judge'll just pin the badge on somebody who will come after you."

"That'd be his hard luck."

"Why don't you lock me in a cell?" Homer suggested. "Then everybody'll know I couldn't have stopped you."

"Is that how you want it?"

"Well, yeah," he said. "I don't wanna have to go up against you. If you're gonna kill 'im, hell, leave town right after you do. By the time somebody finds me in here, you'll be long gone. And if nobody sees you do it, nobody'll know. Then, how could the judge send me after *you*?"

"All right," she said, with a shrug. "Let's go put you in a cell."

Chapter Forty-Five

After locking the sheriff in his own jail cell Roxy left the building by the back door. She made her way through the streets, drawing some attention, but none from anyone who could do her harm. Let them look, she thought.

When she got to Edward Sughrue's house, she walked around it first, peering in the windows, until she spotted him, sitting on a sofa and holding a drink. She then went to the back door, which she assumed would be the easier one to force. But halfway there, she decided to go right to the front door and knock. She wanted to see the look on Sughrue's face when he opened it and saw her.

She went to the front, up onto the porch, and knocked on the door. He didn't answer. Since she knew he was inside, she knocked again, this time harder.

When the door opened, a haggard Edward Sughrue looked out at her. She was disappointed that his face showed nothing—no shock, no surprise.

"What do you want?" he asked. "I thought you left town a long time ago."

"I did," Roxy said. "I'm back."

"I suppose you want to come in." He didn't wait for an answer, just turned and walked away.

She entered the house and closed the door behind her.

Sughrue was back on the sofa, pouring himself another drink. Then he looked at her and spread his arms, spilling a bit of whiskey from the glass as he did.

"Is this what you wanted to see?" Sughrue asked. "What I do, day and night? I sit here and drink. That's what I've been doing since you and your friend hung my boy."

"That's what he gets for killing someone."

"He was a boy."

"He was old enough to kill," Roxy said. "And now you've sent more men to bushwhack Angela Blackthorne, and she's dead."

His blurry eyes fixed on her in that moment.

"If she's dead, good," he said. "But I didn't send anyone to bushwhack her. Why would I? The deed's done."

"First, you did it to try and stop her," Roxy said. "Now you've done it for revenge."

"So you're here to, what?" he asked. "Kill me? Get your revenge? Go ahead, see if I care. If I had the courage, I'd kill myself."

She studied him for a moment, then asked, "How'd you get out of jail?"

"The sheriff opened the cell door and told me the judge told him to do it."

"So tell me, Sughrue," Roxy said, "if you didn't send a bunch of men to ambush Angie Blackthorne, who did?"

"How would I know? Go ask the judge."

"What reason would the judge have?" Roxy asked.

"What reason did he have to release me and not charge me?" Sughrue asked. "Oh, here's one. How about he wanted to bushwhack the Blackthorne woman and have me get the blame?"

"That doesn't figure, Sughrue," she said. "Nothing figures but that you did it."

"Well, if you're dead sure of that," he said, "then shoot me. Do it now."

He poured another drink. He could feel, just under his thigh, the .45 he had been keeping on the sofa for the past few weeks, intending one night to blow his own head off, as soon as he got the nerve. Now he thought it would just be easier to wait for Lady Gunsmith to do it for him. Then, suddenly, as he drank, he grew angry. Why should this woman be allowed to come into his home and take his life, when she and her friend had already taken his son's? No, there had to be another way.

With his glass in his left hand, he reached down for the gun with his right.

***

Sheriff Homer was nobody's fool.

Just in case he ever got locked in one of his own cells, he kept a key hidden in each one, secreted beneath each pallet. No prisoner had ever found one, yet. After Roxy Doyle left the office, he reached underneath the pallet, grabbed the key and let himself out.

Strapping on his gun, he left the office and went right to Judge Tyler's chambers.

"Why do you look so frazzled, Sheriff?" the judge asked, as he entered.

"She's back!"

"Who's back?"

"Lady Gunsmith."

"Is she alone?"

"Yes, she says the other woman, Blackthorne, is dead. She was bushwhacked."

Judge Tyler sat back in his chair.

"So where is she now?"

"She went to Mr. Sughrue's house. I think she's gonna kill 'im."

"Good," Tyler said. "Sughrue is the last link to Copper City. Once he's gone, we'll change the name of the town and move on."

"But . . . what about her?"

"After she kills him, she'll ride out," Tyler said. "She'll never know it was me who sent the men to ambush Blackthorne."

"I still can't figure that, Judge," Homer said. "Why'd you do it?"

"For exactly this reason," Tyler said. "So she'd come back here and kill Sughrue."

"So what do you want me to do?"

"I want you to do exactly what you're good at, Sheriff," Tyler said. "Nothing! That's all! Get out!"

Sheriff Homer left the judge's chamber feeling the sting of the man's words. He felt Copper City would not only benefit from Edward Sughrue being killed, but Judge Tyler, as well.

***

Roxy was watching Sughrue carefully. He seemed like a wasted husk of a man, but in her experience rich men stubbornly hung on to their egos. Even in the face of his son's death, his desire for vengeance could not go unquenched.

"So you're telling me I should go kill Judge Tyler if I want revenge."

"That's what I'm telling you," he said, slurring his words.

It was also her experience that men who drank did not suddenly start slurring their words, it was a gradual progression to that point. He must've been faking.

"All right," she said, "I'll go and see the judge."

She turned to leave. As she did, he grabbed the gun beneath his thigh and started to bring it around. Roxy drew her gun cleanly and fired before Sughrue could. He dropped it, and his glass, as the bullet struck him, and he slid to the floor.

Roxy walked over and looked down at him. His eyes were fluttering. She leaned over.

"Tell me, Sughrue," she said, "you sent those men, didn't you?"

"I . . . did . . . not!" he said, haltingly, yet firmly. "It—it had to be the judge."

"Why would he do it?" she asked.

"Ask him," Sughrue said, "before you k-kill him!"

As the man died, she thought that didn't sound like a bad idea.

Chapter Forty-Six

Roxy left Sughrue's house by the front door. It was far enough away from the other houses in the area that nobody heard the shot. But when she stepped out, she was surprised to see the sheriff standing there.

"Now, hold on," he said, quickly raising his hands. "I just wanna talk."

"How'd you get out of that cell?"

"I had a key hidden," he said. "I ain't a complete idiot."

"What's on your mind?"

"I heard the shot," Homer said. "Is he dead?"

"He is."

"You know, he's not the one who sent those men after Blackthorne."

He told me it wasn't him," Roxy said, "but he pulled a gun on me. I had to shoot."

"I don't have a problem with that," Homer said. "But I thought you'd wanna know who did send those men."

"Judge Tyler."

"That's right," Sheriff Homer said. "Sughrue told you that, too?"

"That was his best guess."

"Well, he was right," Homer said. "The judge wanted you to come back here and kill Sughrue."

"Why?"

"He's lookin' to change the name of the town," Homer said, "and Sughrue is the last link to Copper City."

"Not a good reason to want a man dead," Roxy said.

"So what will you do? Kill the judge?"

"I can't just walk in there and shoot him," Roxy said. "He's a judge."

"Well," Homer said, "I have an idea . . ."

***

Roxy waited on the porch of Sughrue's house, and eventually Sheriff Homer appeared with Judge Tyler in tow.

"I don't understand why I had to come to his house," Tyler was saying. "What's gotten into you?"

"I just thought there was somethin' here you'd wanna see, Judge," Homer said.

"What, Sughrue's dead body?"

"No," Roxy said, stepping out where the judge could see her, "me."

The judge stared at her, then looked at Homer and asked, "What is this?"

"An ambush," Homer said. "Isn't that what you deal in, Judge?"

"You told her?" Tyler asked the lawman.

"Actually," Roxy said, "Sughrue told me. That is, he told me he didn't do it, and the only other logical choice was you."

"So what now? You kill me? I'm a judge, goddamnit."

"I know that," Roxy said. "But what else would you have me do?"

"Is Sughrue really dead?" Tyler asked.

"He is."

"Then that should be the end of it," he said. "He's the one who started the whole bushwhack business."

"And you finished it," Roxy said. "Or, rather, I am."

"You can't shoot me," Tyler warned her again. "I'm unarmed."

"Here ya go, Judge," Homer said, taking his gun from his holster. He put it down on the railing right next to the judge, within easy reach.

"This is murder," Judge Tyler said. "I'm no gunman."

"This isn't murder, Judge," Roxy said, "it's justice. And I have a witness to prove it wasn't an ambush."

"Homer," the judge said, "you're crazy. You can't let this happen."

"He can't do anything else, if he wants to deserve that badge," Roxy said. "A man like you can't be allowed to stay on the bench, Judge. You don't deserve it."

She was beginning to doubt he would go for the gun, so she decided to give him a chance. Sheriff Homer was standing off to the side, and she deliberately turned to face him.

"Sheriff, why don't you—"

The judge reached for the gun as quickly as he could. That was all Roxy needed. She drew and fired. The bullet struck him in the chest and drove him off the porch, as if he had been yanked from behind.

She stepped down and leaned over him, determined that he was dead. Then she turned quickly, in case the sheriff had decided to take a hand. But he was just standing there, watching.

"Now Copper City can grow," he said, "without having to bend to the will of these two crazy men."

"I don't care," Roxy said, replacing the ejected empty shell and holstering her gun. "I'm done, so you can do what you want."

Homer retrieved his gun and holstered it as Roxy walked away.

"Where's your horse?" he asked.

"It's a few miles walk from here," she said. "I don't mind."

She walked a few feet more, then turned and looked at him.

"If you tell this story differently, and somebody comes after me, I'll be back for you."

"No," Homer said, "we made a deal. Your task is done, and mine's beginnin'."

She nodded, turned and walked away.

Coming November 27, 2020!

A Special Christmas Edition

THE GUNSMITH GIANT
THE JINGLE BELL TRAIL

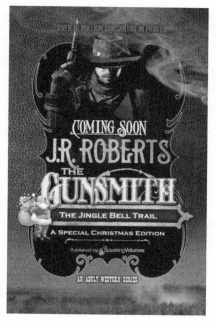

Clint Adams follows the jingle bell trail to a town where he brings Christmas cheer to a widowed mother and her little boy.

**For more information
visit:** www.SpeakingVolumes.us

Coming Spring 2021!

Lady Gunsmith
Book 10
Roxy Doyle and the
Queen of the Pasteboards

Lottie Deno is one of the most famous gamblers of the Old West, making her name in various Texas towns. But in 1877 she and her man, Frank, moved to Kingston, New Mexico where they ran a gambling room in the Victorio Hotel…

It seems some men have come to town to draft Lottie into playing for them in a big poker tournament, and if she doesn't, they'll kill her husband, who they have kidnapped. It falls to Roxy to get Lottie out of the situation…

For more information

visit: www.SpeakingVolumes.us

On Sale Now!

Lady Gunsmith *series*
Books 1 – 8

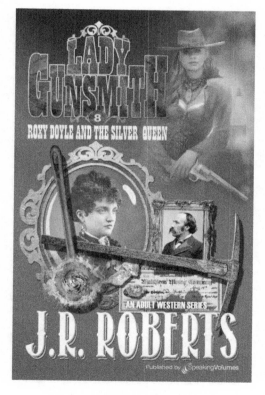

For more information
visit:

On Sale Now!

THE GUNSMITH *series*
Books 430 - 462

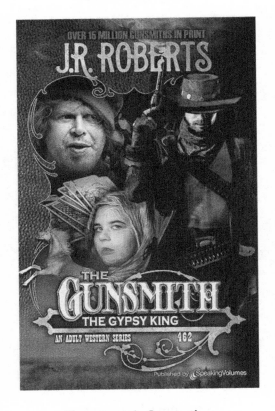

For more information
visit: www.SpeakingVolumes.us

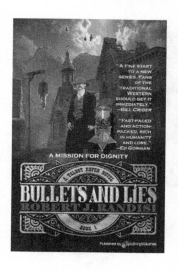

On Sale!

Award-Winning Author
Robert J. Randisi (J.R. Roberts)

For more information
visit: www.SpeakingVolumes.us

Sign up for free and bargain books

Join the Speaking Volumes mailing list

Text

ILOVEBOOKS

to 22828 to get started.

Made in the USA
Monee, IL
16 April 2022